THE HORSE

Also by Willy Vlautin

The Night Always Comes

Don't Skip Out on Me

The Free

Lean on Pete

Northline

The Motel Life

THE HORSE

A Novel

WILLY VLAUTIN

HARPER

An Imprint of HarperCollins*Publishers*

THE HORSE. Copyright © 2024 by Willy Vlautin. All rights reserved. Printed in the United States of America. No part of this book may be used or reproduced in any manner whatsoever without written permission except in the case of brief quotations embodied in critical articles and reviews. For information, address HarperCollins Publishers, 195 Broadway, New York, NY 10007.

HarperCollins books may be purchased for educational, business, or sales promotional use. For information, please email the Special Markets Department at SPsales@harpercollins.com.

FIRST EDITION

Designed by Leah Carlson-Stanisic

Library of Congress Cataloging-in-Publication Data has been applied for.

ISBN 978-0-06-3346574

24 25 26 27 28 LBC 5 4 3 2 1

For John Doe

In memory of Dallas Good

"The only way to get through school is to disappear into a song. Just hum it to yourself and you'll be okay. If you hate being home, hate it here, just disappear into a song. It works, man, I'm telling you it really works."

—*A fifteen-year-old friend of my brother's talking to me in my mom's house when I was eleven*

THE HORSE

1

The board-and-batten walls of the single-room shack that was the assayer's office rattled from the wind, and the fire in the stove was dead. From a twin bed, Al Ward, sixty-seven years old, bone-thin, with gray hair and blue eyes, looked out the window to falling snow. He pulled the blankets and sleeping bag over his head and tried again to sleep but sleep wouldn't come. In the darkness he asked himself the same question he asked every morning. If he were in Reno, eating breakfast at the Cal Neva, would he order coffee, French toast, and bacon like a normal person or a Hornitos on the rocks? The same question and always the same answer: tequila on the rocks with a beer back.

He pushed off the covers and looked at the empty wood-bin. The shack was frozen because he had a cracked woodstove that burned too fast and he hadn't brought in enough wood. But that was the way of mornings. Tequila instead of breakfast and Al staring at the empty woodbin, cursing himself until his bladder forced the day upon him.

The days on the derelict mining claim were always the same. He'd bring in firewood, drink coffee and eat breakfast, work on a song, take a nap, drink more coffee, and then set out on the same walk he took each afternoon. Dinner at dusk, which at that point was four p.m., and afterward he'd play guitar until he grew tired. He'd then get back in bed and read ten-year-old issues of *National Geographic* and *Sports Illustrated* by the light of a propane lantern and chase radio stations on a small battery-powered radio.

A day and a night.

The clock next to his bed read 6:33 a.m. Why couldn't he sleep until noon like he had most of his life? If he could, then half of his day would be over by the time he opened his eyes. But in old age he had trouble sleeping. He slept in fits and woke early, exhausted but awake. Everyone said getting up was easier the older you got, but that hadn't been the case in his life. It was a brawl each morning just to get his feet on the ground.

In wool socks and long underwear, he put on sweats, tennis shoes, and a canvas coat and walked outside carrying a plastic milk crate. Snow and wind blew into him and he made four trips to the shed to fill the woodbin. He started a fire and poured water into a saucepan from a two-gallon jug sitting on a shelf above the sink. He lit a Coleman propane camping stove and set the saucepan on it. The counter where the stove sat was made of two-by-fours and plywood and had a stainless-steel sink that drained through a PVC pipe down under the floor into a washout of mine tailings below. The assayer's shack had no electricity or running water. The toilet was an outhouse behind the shed.

On another shelf was a ceramic dish that held a silver wristwatch and two rings: a silver horseshoe with fake rubies that he put on his left index finger, and a silver horseshoe with fake diamonds that he put on his right. He took off his sweats, set them under the covers of the bed, and dressed in a pair of Levi's and a black-and-red-plaid Pendleton wool shirt. He brushed his teeth and, when the water had heated, made instant coffee.

A butterscotch-blond Telecaster sat under his bed, and leaned against a wall was a classical six-string guitar with a dented back that he'd gotten from a thrift shop in Las Vegas. At a Formica table near the woodstove, he worked on a song called "The Night the Primadonna Club Burned Down," the lyrics written in a spiral notebook. There were a dozen of these notebooks stacked in a cardboard box in the corner of the room. Above the lyrics he had scribbled *Uncle Vern*, *swimming in the river*, *Vern and Gail*, *Primadonna Club*, and a list of dates he had worked on the song.

As a kid his uncle Vern had been a goofball with no real rebellion or anger in him. In high school he'd played football in the fall and run track in the spring. He got decent grades and had a steady girlfriend named Shelby Rosen. When he graduated, his father helped get him on a line crew with the Southern Pacific Railroad, a union job he both liked and felt lucky to have.

During his first working year, he lived at home and slept in his same childhood room. When the second year came, he took a vacation to Tempe to see Shelby at Arizona State. He asked her to marry him at a Mexican restaurant called El Charro in Phoenix, and she accepted. The plan was that she would finish that term of college, they'd get married, and she'd get her degree in Reno. Vern came home so excited that he rented them a one-bedroom house off Wells Avenue, moved in, and waited.

But he had never lived on his own, and as the year passed he became increasingly lonely. He began going out with a coworker to the bars and casinos of downtown Reno. Vern, who had never had a sip of alcohol in his life, began to drink. When Shelby returned to Reno that summer she ended their relationship after he had arrived to three of her family functions intoxicated. That following winter he was terminated from Southern

Pacific Railroad for drunkenness. His bosses had given him three warnings and had sent him to a company doctor. His bosses liked him, but the doctor deemed Vern incurable and he was let go. By twenty-three he had been fired from a half-dozen jobs and began the life of a day laborer. By twenty-six he had lost both parents and settled into washing dishes in casino restaurants and living in a weekly motel east of downtown called the Sandman.

A mile from that motel, Al and his mother lived in a duplex she owned on Humboldt Street, they on one side and a tenant on the other. Each unit had a bedroom, a bathroom, a kitchen, a living room, and a basement. Their basement was Al's bedroom, a cramped concrete box of a room with a utility sink, a dresser, a desk, a bed, and two small windows below the ceiling.

During the summer, when Al was a kid and out of school, Vern would stop by and they'd go to the river to swim. On the way they would buy two quarts of beer and a bottle of Orange Crush and go south of the River House Motor Hotel to a place on the Truckee River shaded with cottonwood trees and a deep pool for swimming. His uncle would be haggard and undone. He'd sit on a flat rock at the river's edge and speak in rambling half-thought-out sentences. But after the first quart and the first swim, he'd begin to recover. A window would appear, a clarity would come, and Vern would again be himself.

"Tell me what you did yesterday."

"Nothing."

"Nothing?"

"I just walked around downtown," Al said.

"All day?"

"I guess."

"Who did you see?"

"I don't know."

"Did you see Jimmy the Broom?"

"Yeah."

"Does he still have a black eye?"

Al nodded.

"Shit, I can't believe someone would hit an old guy for sweeping a sidewalk. But that's people for you." Vern looked at Al and smiled. "Man, I'm stuck washing dishes, and you got no job, and you get to walk around downtown all summer seeing people. You live the life."

Al nodded.

"Why are you so quiet, then?"

Al shrugged.

"You get in trouble?"

"I don't know."

"What did you do, cough too loud?"

"She's never happy with anything," Al whispered.

Vern took a long drink of beer. "Yeah, I know that."

"Why?"

"Well, you know what they say about chicks who get on the straight and narrow?"

Al looked at him. "What do they say?"

"That they leave every bit of their goodtime in the backseat. I mean the only friend your mom's got is a nun, and you know them. They wear the black-and-white underwear, and they spend their time looking for people like you and me to beat up on. That's the truth . . . Shit, Al . . . Your mom . . . Well . . . Someone grabbed her goodtime and ran off with it."

Al dove into the river and swam around and then got onto a rock across from Vern and lay in the sun. But by then Vern was halfway through the second quart and the window began to close. By midday a new quart would be bought and Vern's words would slur, his sentences would fall apart, and his logic would again fade. By evening he would be incoherent and stumbling drunk.

He was nearly beaten to death in an alley off Virginia Street when he was twenty-seven. His wallet and room key were stolen, the hearing in his right ear was damaged, his face battered. He never again looked the same. There was still a handsomeness to him, but the beating had aged him. His youthfulness, the hope that he might pull out of it someday, began to disappear.

Two years later the phone in the duplex rang at three a.m. It had never rung that late before. Al's mother was on the phone less than five minutes. He could hear her footsteps in the kitchen afterward and could smell coffee brewing. He put on his clothes and went upstairs. His mother was in her robe smoking a cigarette, crying. Vern had been found robbed and beaten to death in an alley behind the El Cortez Hotel. Whoever had done it had taken his wallet, his boots, and even his wool coat.

After months of him working on "The Night the Primadonna Club Burned Down," it had become the imagined romance between Vern and a cocktail waitress named Gail, named after the alcoholic actress Gail Russell. In the song she worked at the Primadonna Club, and it was there that she met and fell in love with Vern. They rented a house and moved in together. But one night the club's owner attacked her in a coat-check room. She came home sobbing, her uniform ripped and her underwear gone.

Vern waited a month and then robbed and burned the Primadonna Club to the ground. He and Gail left for San Francisco by train and lived in a suite at the Fairmont Hotel. They were never caught, never went broke, never became punch-drunk, and were always in love. Al wrote and crossed out lyrics and finally leaned the guitar against the table and fell back onto his bed. Jesus, he missed Vern. If there was one person besides Maxine he had never recovered from losing, it was him.

Vern had been Al's best friend and besides Mel, later on, his only father figure. He was an undependable drunk but he had never judged or criticized Al. He always just seemed happy to see him. His whole face would light up when he did, like it was the best thing in his life just to see Al.

Outside the snow continued. Al got up from bed and stood next to the stove. He took off his Pendleton shirt and jeans and hung them from nails on the wall next to his bed. The rings were set back in the dish on the shelf above the sink, and he put on a pair of thick mechanic coveralls, his boots and canvas coat, and a bright orange ski cap and went outside.

2

The mine was in the high desert of central Nevada at 6,500 feet. It was thirty miles from the nearest ranch and fifty miles from the nearest town, Tonopah. On the porch outside the assayer's office, a rusted Chevron thermometer read ten degrees. Al went down the porch steps into an already darkening day. Snow dusted the canyon walls and gravel road, the wind blew, and he began the same walk he did each day: a mile to the remnants of the last miner's house and back.

In the early 1900s more than three hundred men had worked and lived at the mine. They had built makeshift homes along the canyon walls. Over the following decades the mine had opened and closed four different times before being decommissioned in 1956 and left abandoned.

Al passed the fragments of three different brick buildings and then the mine itself, where a yellow engineless 1960s school bus was shoved vertically into the main shaft. On the opposite side of the canyon were the remains of a half-dozen other buildings. Below them, pushed into a gulley, was a burned-out 1980s travel trailer that his great-uncle Mel and his dog, Curly, had escaped from one night when its propane heater had caught fire.

It was dusk when Al made it to the last structure, a wooden storage shed caved into itself. He took a pocketknife from his coat and notched a line into a four-by-four stud next to over eighteen hundred other small notches. For nearly five years he had done this same walk. Every day he wasn't too sick or depressed or the weather didn't forbid him, he walked.

The woodshed next to the assayer's office was half full of cottonwood, pine, and aspen logs. Al made three trips filling the woodbin by the stove. He then carried his spare two-gallon water jug to the spring twenty yards behind the office. Underneath a metal cover he dipped the jug into the four-foot-round concrete pipe his great-uncle had installed. Why it never froze completely, Al didn't know, but even when the temperature was below zero, only a thin layer of ice covered the spring water.

Inside he took off his coat and coveralls, put his sweats back on, relit the woodstove, and sat in the duct-taped vinyl recliner next to it. In a spiral notebook he worked on the lyrics to a song called "Black Thoughts I Only See." Above the title he had written *Mexicali, Dog, The Falling Apart Years, The Wall.* The band he was in at the time, the Gold 'n Silver Gang, had been on the road for two weeks when they stopped at the Little Acorn Casino outside of Campo, California, for a three-night engagement. The morning of the second day the band decided to drive to the border town of Mexicali. The band members, all under thirty, wanted to find a red-light district. Al, who had just turned fifty-six, had no interest and decided to walk the streets of Mexicali as a tourist.

He drank daytime beers, looked in shops, and sat for a long time in a courtyard. For lunch he ate at a sidewalk restaurant on the edge of the tourist area. It was then that he saw a dog across the street. A mutt-shepherd that was brown and black and white in color and had one ear that stood up and one that flopped over. He watched the dog as it lay down in the shade of a white stucco building, panting in the midday heat. Even as cars drove by and people passed, the dog stared at Al and Al stared at the dog. But his meal came and he ate and soon he forgot about the dog across the street.

It was hours later, as he headed toward the border gate to meet the band, that he saw it again. By then he had gone in and out of a half-dozen stores, drunk in two bars, and crossed a dozen streets. He stood near the twenty-foot-tall rust-colored border fence, knelt down, and invited the dog to him. And the dog came. It had mange and was underweight, one of its eyes was clouded with goo, and it had a thick pink scar along its muzzle.

Al spoke to the dog and began to pet it along its neck. The dog licked his arm. Time stopped. It was as though the dog and Al were the only ones alive. The chaos and sadness of the outside world disappeared around them. They were just there, together. But a group of American tourists passed. The sidewalk was narrow and a man with a walker bumped into Al and an obese woman in a pink Disneyland T-shirt, white pants, and tennis shoes brushed against the mutt and screamed.

The dog ran off.

Al decided then he would save it. He would bring the dog back with him. So instead of going to the van to meet the band at the scheduled time, he turned from the border gate and headed back into Mexicali. For two hours he frantically searched the streets and alleys and courtyards, but he never again saw the dog. It had vanished. When he got back to the van, the band members wouldn't speak to him. He was docked a hundred dollars and put on probation, and they barely made it in time to that night's gig.

*   *   *

Al put down the pen and read the lyrics.

BLACK THOUGHTS I ONLY SEE

A man finds a dog in Mexicali, Mexico, half dead and starving
He sneaks it across the border hidden in his truck
For months he nurses it back from dying
But the dog has never trusted anyone and escapes the first
   chance he sees
The man stays up all night worried and searching
The dog wants to go back to the man but gets lost in the gullies
Three days on the run and he gets shot by some kids hunting
He hides in the brush and cries for the man, the only friend in
   his life he's ever seen
While the man puts up flyers in laundromats and stores and
   always keeps searching
Black thoughts are again haunting me
Black thoughts I only see
Black thoughts, a bottle, and memories of Maxine

It was dusk when he woke. The day was over. The recliner
creaked as he stood, and outside the wind continued to howl.
He opened a can of Campbell's condensed chicken noodle soup,
put it in a saucepan, added water, and heated it on the Coleman
stove. He ate and loaded the stove with wood and got into bed
and read *National Geographic* by the light of the lantern.

3

At three a.m. he woke. He turned the radio on and found a Mexican station out of Las Vegas, and Los Tigres del Norte played "*Contrabando y Traición.*" It was a tune he knew well, and in the polka sound of the accordion he tried to breathe and disappear into the song's story: a corrido about a couple, a man and a woman, who sneak drugs across the U.S. border. They drive to Los Angeles and sell the drugs, get the money, and don't get caught. They win. But the man tells the woman he's leaving her, that he has another girlfriend in the States. A girlfriend who is his true love. The woman is so blindsided and devastated that she shoots the man, takes the money, and runs.

By the time the song ended, Al was wide awake and his mind fell to the darkness that had plagued him each night at that time for as long as he could remember. He had heard that if you didn't have a job, if you were alone and at home, the suicide hour was two p.m. The middle of the day, hours before night and the relief of sleep. A time of heat and exhaustion in the summer, and lethargy and loneliness in winter. But for Al, the suicide hour had always been three a.m. The night prison, he called it.

His second wife, Maxine, had told him that when the night prison found her she would force herself to get up and either watch TV or go to the kitchen and eat. She told him that nothing good came from staying in bed and having darkness lead you down one hall and then another and another until you were lost.

But Al knew thinking of Maxine was only another room in his night prison, so he lit the bedside lantern. He put on his tennis shoes and headlamp and went outside to find the sky clear and blanketed with stars. He made two trips for wood, started a fire, and put water on for coffee. He changed into his Levi's and Pendleton shirt, put the rings on his fingers, and sat at the table with his guitar, a notebook, and a cup of coffee. He worked on a half-finished song called "The Night Buck Owens Came to Town." In the right corner of the page he had written 14-14-14, *Pontiac Grand Prix, 1959–'60,* and *Me and Mom in the Kitchen.*

At fourteen Al was six feet three inches tall, his hair jet black, and his eyes light blue. His face was dotted with acne and he weighed a hundred and thirteen pounds. His body was his constant embarrassment. Just undressing in P.E. revealed to all the rivers of blue veins under his skin and the bones of his skeletal frame.

Fourteen was also the year he experienced his first prolonged mental anguish over the death of his uncle Vern. Within a week of hearing the news he became paralyzed in a sort of panic fit that wouldn't abate. He couldn't sleep and had no appetite or energy. Vern had been not only his uncle but also his best friend and only confidant. His mother had refused to talk about her brother, so Al never told her or anyone how broken he was by the loss or admitted the panic and sadness that followed his uncle's death.

Fourteen was also the year his mother's part-time boyfriend,

14 WILLY VLAUTIN

Herb Marks, stopped in front of the duplex in a white Pontiac Grand Prix. From the kitchen window Al and his mother saw him pull up, and Al grabbed his coat and left. Inside, the car was warm and had a white leather interior and clear plastic floor mats covering white carpet. Herb, a bulky bald man with a waxed mustache, owned three auto-parts stores and smoked two cigarettes on the drive to John Ascuaga's Nugget to see Buck Owens and the Buckaroos.

This was years before Buck was "Hee Haw Owens," but even so the casino's smaller main-floor lounge was full, and the band came to the stage in sparkling blue Nudie suits. Buck grinned his big white toothy smile and said witty things between songs. The Buckaroos played with a sort of controlled abandon and Buck acted like he was the happiest man who had ever lived on earth.

Maybe it was because Al's mother and Vern had always had the country station on, or maybe it was because he'd never been to a live music show before, but seeing Buck Owens that night became a marker for everything after. It wasn't the suits or the adulation that came from being onstage that attracted him. Nor the idea of money or fame. It was that when they played, he disappeared. When they played, suddenly Al wasn't Al anymore. He was transported inside the noise and rhythm and melody and story. It was as though suddenly he understood that just by a song playing he was able to vanish from himself.

A month later he came home from school to find his mother and Herb sitting in the backyard. On the picnic table was a 1959 butterscotch-blond Telecaster guitar, a guitar cord, and a Fender Princeton amp. "You got the bug. I can tell," Herb said in his smoker's voice. "I had these in my garage breeding dust.

They're yours if you want them. All you gotta do is learn to play and you'll be famous in no time."

"You're giving them to me?" Al looked at his mother.

His mother nodded and Al ran to the table. The next day, after school, he checked out *Sing 'N' Strum Guitar Method and Song Folio* and *The Folksinger's Guitar Guide: An Instruction Manual* from the library and he practiced every moment he could. His mother told him she was surprised he didn't shower with the guitar. He ate breakfast and dinner with it on his lap, he watched TV with it, and he spent hours each night in his basement room playing along to the radio. He bought music magazines and read about Lefty Frizzell, Hank Cochran, Merle Haggard, the Everly Brothers, and later on Bob Dylan and the Rolling Stones.

At seventeen he answered an ad in the *Reno Gazette* and joined his first band, a weekend casino country covers group called Bobbi Blue and the Bonnevilles, led by a twenty-two-year-old waitress named Bobbi Holms. The four-piece band practiced in a garage in Sparks, and from their very first rehearsal Al was overcome with the joy of it. His ears rang from his guitar amp and the sound of the drums and cymbals banging away next to him. He was in a band.

Bobbi Blue and the Bonnevilles played local casinos for over a year, and eventually Al showed them a tune he'd written, a rave-up rockabilly number called "Roll Reno Roll." Their manager, a local restaurant equipment salesman, wanted them to record it. A hundred singles were pressed, and for two weeks the song was played in rotation on the local country radio station. When Al heard "Roll Reno Roll" for the first time on his basement radio he openly wept. After that he would have played with Bobbi Blue and the Bonnevilles for the rest of his life if Bobbi hadn't gotten married and quit music toward the end of his senior year in high school.

ROLL RENO ROLL

I got nowhere to go
I got no money and I got no home
The highway, man, is flashing by
I'm whipping through the mountains
To those casino lights
They're Paris to me, man, and Istanbul
They're Hollywood and Budapest and Tokyo
I'll get on a roll and that roll will never slow
Roll Reno Roll
Roll Reno Roll
I ain't gonna fall, buddy, I'm gonna rise
I ain't gonna fail, buddy, I'm gonna fly
Roll Reno Roll
Roll Reno Roll
Come on man let's go
Roll Reno Roll

Al got up from the table, leaned his guitar against the wall, and heated a can of Campbell's vegetable soup on the Coleman stove. He took off his Levi's and Pendleton shirt, set the rings in the dish, put more wood in the stove, and got back in bed. The sun began its rise over the mountains and Al thumbed through *Atlas of the Breeding Birds of Nevada*, read about the Forster's tern, and fell asleep. The day passed and he woke an hour before dusk. He took his walk, ate, and got back in bed.

4

A horse stood in the middle of the road outside the assayer's office the next morning. It was sorrel in color and stood motionless in the morning light. Even from inside, twenty yards away, Al could see that something hung from the horse's left eye. Dressed in his sweats, he put on his boots and coat and went outside. The sky was cloudless and blue and the sun had just begun to hit the tops of the canyon walls. The horse didn't move, only its breath quickened as Al approached. He could now see its left eye was completely swollen shut, the socket encrusted with dried blood and dirt and bits of sagebrush. The right eye was also swollen closed and caked with wet and dried yellow mucus.

The horse was blind.

Al bent down and took a handful of snow and put it to his face. He closed his eyes, thinking the horse wasn't real, that somehow he was still asleep. But when he opened them again, it was there. A blind horse. Its mane matted and tangled with sagebrush, its body littered with scars. A half-inch-wide one ran the entire length of its belly, a decaying racing stripe. Other scars were on its legs, on its neck and withers, and a faded brand read *Tt* on its left hip.

Al knew nothing of horses. Never once had he ridden one, and he couldn't remember having ever touched one. As a kid he had never gone to camp or to somebody's ranch. He couldn't recall having even seen one up close. In a half daze he stared at the horse until his feet began to freeze. He then made three trips to the woodshed, started a fire in the stove, and changed into his thermal-lined coveralls. He moved his recliner in front of the window and watched the horse. He drank coffee and waited. But morning turned to midday and the horse didn't move on.

There was an extra five-gallon plastic jug in the woodshed. Al cut it in half with a handsaw. He filled it with water from the spring and brought it to the horse and set it down. The horse's breath again quickened, and in worry it rocked its head back and forth, but it didn't move. Al could see its hooves caked in snow, its thick red winter coat, and the white line that ran between its eyes like a small lightning bolt.

He went back inside, sat in the recliner, and watched. Every so often the horse moved its head down and licked snow off the ground, but it didn't seem to notice the jug and never once drank from it. The day went on, Al grew warm in the coveralls and from the warmth of the fire and fell asleep.

When he opened his eyes, he hoped more than anything that the horse would be gone. But when he looked out the window, the horse was still there, its head down in sleep, a small pile of manure behind its back legs. Al opened a can of Campbell's condensed chicken wonton soup and heated it in a saucepan. He changed out of his coveralls, put more wood in the stove, and ate while sitting in the recliner. Night came and again he fell asleep. When he woke next, it was three a.m., the stove was out, and he was shivering cold. The first thought that came to him was the horse. He grabbed a flashlight and pointed it out the window to see nothing but the white of a snowstorm. A relief came to him. Maybe the horse was gone. He put on his boots and went outside to see it still there, standing in the same spot, its mane now half covered in snow.

No sound came from the canyon. It was completely silent. The water in the bucket had a film of ice over it. He broke it out, and the horse stomped its left leg in worry but didn't move away. Al went back inside and relit the stove and decided when it grew light he'd get his car running and drive the thirty miles to Morton's ranch and get help from Lonnie. He kept the lantern lit, made instant coffee, and sat in the recliner and waited for sunrise.

More than anything he hoped that the horse would be gone by then or would prove to have never been real in the first place. Because Al knew there was a possibility that he was losing his mind. He had begun to feel and see things that weren't real. He'd felt a mountain lion following him for weeks when he'd never seen a sign of one, not even a footprint. And he had begun, on occasion, to see Maxine. There were times when he saw her on his daily walks and times when she came to him at night in the assayer's office. Times when he was certain she was real, and when he saw her he would beg for her forgiveness and he would beg for her to talk to him and live there with him. But when he would do such things, she would only disappear.

A spiral notebook was wedged between the cushion and armrest, and he picked it up and thumbed through pages. He stopped on a nearly finished ballad called "Mona and the Kid." Above the title he had written: *peanut butter and apricot jam sandwich 1967.*

Mona Heidelberg sang under the name Mona Maverick and had the voice of a weary and busted-up Brenda Lee. She was curvy and blond like an aging Playboy Bunny. With makeup and in the right light she looked to be in her late twenties, but in the morning with no makeup she was every day of the thirty-eight-year-old bulimic alcoholic she had become.

Mona had moved to Reno from Fresno, California, with her manager and boyfriend, Everett Simms, in 1965. He put a four-piece band around her and started the group on the casino circuit of Reno, Winnemucca, Elko, Lake Tahoe, and Las Vegas. The first year 230 gigs were played with the same lineup, but five days before a monthlong residency at Harrah's, their guitar player was arrested for domestic abuse.

Everett struggled to find an emergency replacement until he went to the Nevada Club and came across Al, who was nineteen and in a local country covers band called the All-Nighters. Everett stayed until the set ended, met Al, and arranged an audition the next afternoon.

Dressed in his only suit and borrowing his mother's car, Al parked in front of a two-bedroom apartment on Forest Street and walked to the door with his guitar and amplifier. Everett, a middle-aged portly man with combed-over dyed brown hair, answered and introduced Al to Mona. The three of them sat in the living room. Mona played and sang standard country tunes on an acoustic guitar, and Al followed along and did the solos. They ran songs for half an hour, and then Everett and Mona went into their bedroom and closed the door. When they came out, they offered Al the job with a two-week trial period and a list of seventy songs to learn. The gig was four sets a night, six nights a week. He'd be given a dinner voucher each evening and $250 each Saturday.

For the next three days Al learned the songs he had copies of and bought the records of the ones he didn't. The band had a steel player and a rhythm section, and Mona sang and played acoustic guitar on a dozen tunes. Al showed up on time with five pages of cheat sheets laid out in front of him and faked his way through the first week. The band members and Mona and Everett seemed to like him enough and he was hired permanently. He gave two weeks' notice at his job as a breakfast cook at the Holiday Hotel and was, for the first time, a full-time musician.

But as the months passed and the gigs went on, Al realized that the guys in the band kept their distance. They were older—the youngest, the bass player, was forty-two—and they all had wives and children. They began calling Al "The Kid." For the next year they played Lake Tahoe in the summer, Reno in the fall and spring, and Las Vegas in the winter. If they had any weeks off they'd play Carson City, Elko, and Winnemucca. Al worked 250 nights that first year and made four times the money he would have as a cook. But even after all the gigs played, he felt as though he hardly knew any of the guys in the band. On the road he roomed alone and he didn't drink alcohol. The guys drank together after each gig, while Mona and Everett arrived ten minutes before the first song and left within ten minutes of the last.

In Reno, after a gig, Al went home to his mother's duplex and his basement room. He'd lost track of the few friends he'd had in high school, and as the first year in the band ended, he found himself struggling to get out of bed. The panic and sadness that had first appeared with the death of his uncle Vern reappeared. He began to fall apart mentally. He loved playing guitar for a living but liked little else about the job. The band only played covers, and the people in the casinos where they performed barely watched. Song after song after song and the audience just drank and talked and gambled.

At home there was little comfort because his mother was devastated by his choice of work. She openly wept that he played casinos for a living and chose to live his life the way he did. Part of it was a motherly concern for the uncertainty of a musician's life, but more than anything she was embarrassed by it. She told her coworkers and friends that her son was in college studying business. So Al never admitted to her the struggles he had working for Mona. He just got out of bed, showered and shaved, acted happy, and showed up for work.

And then days before a monthlong residency at Harveys in Lake Tahoe, Everett's appendix burst. He was rushed to the hospital and unable to make the trip, and the band left for Lake Tahoe without him. For six nights they played, and when the last song of the fourth set ended, Mona disappeared, the band went to the bar to celebrate a day off, and Al went back to his room, hung up his gig suit, and began reading a western called *Rodeo Clown*. It was one a.m. and he was making a peanut butter and apricot jam sandwich when he heard a knock on the door. He answered in boxer shorts to see Mona in a blue cocktail dress holding a bottle of Jim Beam and two glasses.

"How's it going, Kid?" she said, and smiled. "Let me in before anyone sees." Al stepped back and Mona came in. She flipped off her high heels, set the whiskey and glasses on the dresser, and looked at his sandwich and the loaf of bread and jars of peanut butter and jam. "Are you really eating PB and J?"

Al put on pants and a shirt. "Do you want one?"

"Jesus, you really are a kid," she said, and sat on the bed. "Why don't you go get us some ice."

He did so and Mona poured two drinks and handed him one. Al had sipped whiskey once before, but he didn't like the taste. If someone handed him a beer he would nurse it, but more than anything he was scared of alcohol. His mother had raised him to believe it was the root of all darkness, and all he had to do was look at his uncle Vern or his great-uncle Mel to know she was telling the truth.

"You're a pretty good guitar player," Mona said. "I've seen better but I've seen a lot worse. And Everett says you write songs."

Al stood near the TV and nodded.

"Don't be so nervous. I'm not here to fire you. You're not in trouble. How many you written?"

"Maybe twenty or so," he whispered.

"Come sit next to me," Mona said, and patted the bed. Al walked to her but sat two feet away. Mona inched closer until her arm touched his. "Can I ask you a question?"

"Sure."

"You a virgin?"

Al didn't answer.

"You been with a lot of girls?"

"No."

"How many?"

Al looked at the carpet. He'd had sex only once, with a cocktail waitress from the Nugget Casino in Carson City. The woman was in her thirties and short and heavy. They had flirted for three nights, and when the band finished the final set of the last night, Al waited for her to get off work. They had a drink and then she took him to her car. They did it in the back, next to a child's car seat. She wore a wedding ring and chewed gum while she was on top of him. His bare ass bouncing on stale Cheerios and cornflakes. The car smelled of sour milk and talcum powder.

Al looked at the carpet. "I was with one girl once."

"That's okay," she said, and her voice softened. "I like that. I like that even more. Can I ask you another question?"

"Yeah."

"Do you think about me?"

Al shrugged.

"I bet you do."

Al nodded.

"Can you keep your mouth shut? Can you do something bad and never tell another soul about it for as long as you live?" She put her hand on Al's leg and left it there. "Because I'll fire you if you tell anyone, and you won't work as a guitar player ever again. Not anywhere."

"Tell about what?"

"I'm gonna let you fuck me." Mona moved her hand up his thigh. "And I'm going to teach you how to do it right. Because I don't fuck like a suburban housewife with an apron and a white picket fence."

"I don't know what that means," he said.

"I'm gonna teach you what it means." She got up, turned off the overhead light, and sat back down on the bed. She had Al stand in front of her. The bedside lamp was lit and she told him to take off his clothes and she watched as he did.

Al drank two glasses of whiskey and they fucked three times that night, and always Mona told him what to do and how to do it. When they finally finished, she ordered two Denver omelets with hash browns and pancakes from room service. It was five a.m. She ate her entire omelet, the hash browns, and most of her pancakes. Al ate what he could and fell back into bed and closed his eyes. He was drunk and his body was tingling and warm and exhausted. It felt like heaven. Mona smoked a cigarette on the edge of the bed and went to the bathroom and closed the door.

Al could hear her vomiting. When she came out, she stumbled back to the bed, fell on top of it naked, and passed out.

Twice more that week she came to his room, always late, always drunk, and always carrying a fifth of Jim Beam. By the third week of her visits to his room at Harveys, Al had fallen in love with Mona Heidelberg. Every thought he had suddenly included her somehow, and every song he wanted to write was for her to sing. The anxiety and panic which had plagued him earlier disappeared, and after the gig each night he would rush back to his room and wait and pace and hope that she would knock.

Their time together was always the same. They drank and fucked and ate in his room. They never went out in public and he never saw her in the daytime or in her room. In bed she would say things like, "Do you think I'm a better singer than Tammy Wynette? . . . Now put it in the bad hole . . . Do you really think I look twenty-nine? . . . Now lick it like it's an ice cream cone . . . Slow down, Kid, just get a rhythm and breathe deep so you don't come so fast like you did last time . . . Grab my wrists harder. I mean really hard . . . Am I better than that stupid girl you were with? Are my tits bigger, is my pussy tighter? . . . Pull my hair harder like you're really mad . . . Am I the best-looking woman you've ever seen? . . . Slap it harder. No, harder, like you hate me!" and when they were done she'd order cheeseburgers or steaks, omelets or patty melts, milkshakes, slices of pie or cake. They'd eat until they collapsed. She'd then wait a half hour and push on Al and ask if he was awake, and if he didn't move, she'd go to the bathroom and puke it all out in the toilet.

When the band came home from Lake Tahoe, they began a local residency at the Horseshoe Casino, and Mona convinced Al to move out of his mother's duplex. She found a one-bedroom apartment three blocks from where she lived with Everett and told Al to rent it. She made a list of things for him to buy: a queen-size bed, high-thread-count sheets, a down comforter, expensive bathroom towels, an Italian coffeemaker, a TV and stereo, a couch, a kitchen table and chairs, and a list of food and drinks to keep stocked in the refrigerator.

All the money Al had saved since joining the band disappeared in less than a month and suddenly he found himself living alone, spending his days watching TV and playing guitar, and waiting for Mona. But Mona rarely came, and when she did, it was only for brief moments while she ran errands. "A quickie, but not too quick, Al," she'd say, and laugh. An hour here and forty-five minutes there and always she was sober, tired, and moody.

When the Reno dates ended, the band did a week run in Elko at the Stockman's Casino. Everett again traveled with the group and Mona told Al she wouldn't be coming to his room that trip. For the first four days she barely even acknowledged him and only criticized his playing. He was too loud or his solo on "Almost Persuaded" was too rock and roll or he blew the change on "You Ain't Woman Enough (To Take My Man)."

But on the fifth night the knock came.

"I saw you talking to that bitch," Mona slurred angrily. She held a half-empty fifth of Jim Beam in her right hand. "You were flirting with that cunt all night."

Al stood in his boxer shorts. "Talking to who?"

Mona walked into the room smelling of perfume, whiskey, and bacon. "The redhead. You were shoving it in my face."

"I don't know who you're talking about?"

"She had two other girls with her."

"Oh, that, that was nothing."

"How old is she?"

"Which one?"

"The redhead with the big tits. You know who I'm talking about. Don't act like you don't know what's going on. How old is she?"

"I don't know. She's in college."

"Did she give you her phone number?"

Al nodded. "She wants guitar lessons. That's what we were talking about. She lives in Reno and goes to UNR and wants to learn to play."

"Let me see."

"See what?"

"The number."

Al went to his wallet and took out a bar napkin with a phone number and the name Ricki above it. She had soft loopy handwriting and had put a heart next to her name. He handed the napkin to Mona and she ripped it into small pieces and threw them on the floor. Her face was red, and when she walked toward Al, he thought she was going to hit him. Instead she dropped to her knees, pulled down his underwear, and put him in her mouth.

"She won't do this as good," Mona told him. "She'll get frigid and corner you with five screaming brats and a mortgage. You'll be selling your guitar for diapers. I'm telling you, Kid, it's the truth."

Al pulled Mona up to him. "You don't understand anything." His voice was so shaky and undone he could barely speak. "I love you, Mona. I love you."

"You don't care," she cried, and tried to push him away. "You think I'm an over-the-hill old bag who can't sing anymore."

"You're the best singer I've ever heard. I love you," he told her. "I'm in love with you."

Tears and mascara leaked down Mona's face, but no longer did she struggle to get away. Now she held on to Al so tight it hurt him.

"I love you," he whispered.

"Do you think about me all the time?"

"All day long."

"And night?"

"And night, too."

"You won't fuck that redheaded bitch."

"No."

"Not ever?"

"No," he said.

"You got it bad for me, don't you?"

"Yes."

Mona took off her dress, and it fell to the floor. She stood in black lace underwear and stumbled as she pulled him to bed. She put him inside her and said, "Say you love me."

"I love you."

"Say that you'd kill for me."

"I'd kill for you."

"Do you love me more than the redhead?"

"I don't even know her."

"Do you love me more than anyone?"

"Yes."

"You better," she moaned, "or I'll ruin you."

It was the next morning when Everett thought of Al's room and borrowed a key from the front desk. He found them in bed, naked and asleep. Al woke to the sound of Everett crying in a chair next to the window. He was dressed in a brown suit, his hands covering his face, his combed-over hair in disarray. Al pushed on Mona. She woke bloated and booze-sick. When she saw Everett, she looked at Al and whispered, "You leave us alone. Okay?"

Al looked for his clothes and Mona picked up her dress and went to the bathroom. When she came out, she said in an upbeat voice, "Honey, don't cry. I was drunk and the Kid's a virgin. I thought it would be a laugh. I mean, Jesus, the Kid means nothing to me. Just nothing. I had a few last night and got that itch and had to scratch it. You know how I get."

Al put on his boots and left the room. He went to the Stockman's restaurant and tried to eat but couldn't. After that he walked to the Greyhound station and wrote down the bus times to Reno in case he was fired. He wandered the streets of Elko and became so distraught that from a pay phone he even called his mother at work just to hear her voice.

A four o'clock showing of *This Property Is Condemned* played at the downtown cinema. Al sat in the back corner, and by the time the film ended, he hoped more than anything that he would be fired. Then he could go back to being the Al Ward he was before Mona. The Al who didn't drink or spend his money the second he got it, who wasn't strung out on a woman twice his age. He wanted a girl like Natalie Wood's character, Alva Starr. Someone his age, someone who, in the end, was only his.

It was dusk when he walked back to the casino showroom. Mona was onstage working out "Ain't Had No Lovin'" by Connie Smith. Everett was sitting at the bar drinking coffee. When he saw Al, he only smiled and told him to learn the new tune, as they were adding it to the set that night.

The Elko run ended. In Reno they did three weeks at Harrah's Casino. Mona didn't come to Al's apartment, and at the gigs she barely noticed him. The band then traveled to Las Vegas for a month at the Riviera Casino. It was there that Al began flirting with a young brunette cocktail waitress. During the band's breaks, he'd stand at the bar and talk to her while she picked up her drink orders.

The knock that time came at two a.m. Mona was carrying a fifth of Jim Beam and a peanut butter and jelly sandwich.

"Who was she?"

"What are you talking about?"

"Don't fuck with me, Kid. You know what I'm talking about." Mona came into the room and set the bottle and sandwich on the dresser.

"The cocktail waitress?"

Mona began pacing. "She'll hate your guts within a year, and you'll be stuck working in a bank for the rest of your life."

"Why do you care?" Al's voice shook, his eyes watered, and his lips quivered. "You don't give a shit about me."

Mona moved toward him. "I had to cut it off, don't you see? You gotta understand, Kid, Everett does everything. The number one thing in my life is I can't lose Everett. He's the reason we're getting two hundred and fifty dates a year. He's my ticket."

Al sat on the bed and began to sob. His nerves had given out. He couldn't sleep or eat, and for the first time in his life he'd gotten drunk on his own. He had walked by the Santa Fe Basque Restaurant and gone inside and drunk four beers and a bourbon.

"Don't cry, Kid," Mona said, and sat next to him. "Because I came to celebrate. I came to tell you that Everett understands. He can't satisfy a woman anymore. All he asks is that we keep it on the down-low. Don't let the boys know. You won't let anyone know, will you?"

Al shook his head and wiped his eyes.

Mona ran her hand through his hair and kissed him. She then got up, opened the bottle, and poured two drinks. Al went to the bathroom. He washed his face and opened his shaving kit and took out a red box with a diamond ring in it. He had sold the savings bonds his great-uncle Mel had given him, one of his guitars, and a Honda motorcycle he kept at his mother's duplex.

When he came out, Mona was sitting on the bed.

He dropped to his knees and opened the box. "Will you marry me?"

Mona laughed at first, but then she kissed him so hard it nearly bruised his lips. "You want me that bad, huh, Kid?"

"Yes," he whispered.

"But honey, we need Everett right now. Without Everett we're sunk."

"But I love you, Mona."

"You poor boy," she said, and began kissing him. "You really would die without me, wouldn't you?"

Three days later, on their night off, Al Ward married Mona Heidelberg at a Las Vegas wedding chapel at four a.m. He had just turned twenty-one, and she was two months shy of forty and stumbling drunk when she signed the marriage papers. It was the only time she wore the ring, but that night, in front of everyone they came across, she showed it off. She openly wept and kept her arm around Al and whispered that she loved him. They celebrated with a bottle of champagne and a breakfast of eggs Benedict and waffles at Caesars twenty-four-hour restaurant but kept the marriage secret.

The band came back to Reno for a residency at Harolds Club, and Everett and Mona came up with a Reno schedule. She would stay with Al twice a week. Those were the days Everett drove back to Fresno to manage the hardware store he still owned and to see his kids from the family he'd had before he met Mona. On their nights together Al and Mona would come home from their gig to Al's apartment and make daiquiris, margaritas, or gin fizzes and a three-a.m. dinner. They would fuck for hours, sleep late, and go to movies or the mall before heading to that night's gig. Mona taught Al how and what to drink, how to dress, and how to hold himself in public.

"Even just going to the dentist, you have to look better than anyone else," she told him. "If you want to be big-time, you gotta dress like you're going someplace amazing. Because if you do, people will think you're going someplace amazing, and most likely, if you keep it up, you will be."

The arrangement went on for over a year, during which time Mona disappeared into bouts of despair over her age, her teeth, which were rotting from the acidity of daily vomiting, her struggles with weight and alcohol, and always over her inability to break out of the casino circuit.

Al wrote her a dozen songs that year, and on their nights together he'd play them for her at his kitchen table. Mona began showing them to Everett, and Everett liked what he heard and began putting them in the band's set. He booked studio time in San Francisco and they recorded five songs: "Living Hard, Living Fast"; "Bonnie Disappeared"; "If You Leave Me I'll Die"; "Waiting on a Bus Out of Town"; "Yesterday I Saw You and Her Walking Down the Street." The session was a success, and after four years of trying, Everett got Mona signed to a subsidiary Nashville label called Roustabout Records.

After that, however, Everett clamped down on Mona. He went home to Fresno only twice a month instead of every week. He also kept her to three drinks a day, she began jogging, and they drove to Oakland and met with a high-end beautician whose expertise was making women look younger.

It was early fall when they finished a monthlong run at Caesars Lake Tahoe, and Everett gathered the band backstage. On a foldout table were four gift baskets, each filled with a fifth of whiskey, a box of chocolates, an assortment of fruit, a tie, and an envelope. "What I have to say is difficult because I like and respect you all so much. Both Mona and I do. I can't begin to tell you how honored we've been to be a part of this group, but I'm afraid this is the end of the line for us as a band." Sweat leaked from Everett's face, and his burgundy suit was wet under the armpits. "I apologize for the lack of warning, but that's just the business we're in. Mona and I have decided to move to Nashville, where the label is located. Although I talked with them about bringing you guys with us, they want to use studio musicians for the recording of Mona's first full-length album. Once we begin promotion, I'll check back in. Some of you, maybe all of you, would like to help take Mona nationally as a part of her road band. But right now all I can say is thank you. I've given each of you a bonus of a thousand dollars. It's in the gift basket on the table. Each basket is personalized with your name. Mona picked out each tie individually and helped put the baskets together. Hopefully the bonus will be of some cushion until you can find another job. Again, thank you and I hope we can stay in touch."

Everett and Mona left and Al carried the basket and his gear to his room. He spent the night waiting and pacing and unable to sleep because Mona had told him none of it. He had absolutely no idea. The next morning he went to Everett and Mona's room to find they had checked out the day before so he caught a ride back to Reno. As soon as he had dropped off his things, he ran to Everett and Mona's apartment to find a for-rent sign on their front door. They had moved out at the beginning of the Caesars run.

He didn't hear from Mona for three months, until he received a letter from Everett, postmarked Nashville, Tennessee, saying Mona wanted a divorce. Al wrote back saying he'd grant the divorce, that all he wanted was to talk to her one last time. Everett said that he would set it up and gave Al the number and address of a local divorce attorney to contact.

"Kid, it hurts me bad the way this has all played out," Mona said when she called. "But you're lucky you're not in Nashville. Everett watches me like a goddamn prison guard. I've begun calling him the Warden. Even if I have to go to the pharmacy or the grocery, Everett's out there warming up the car. My God, he's become a real hoverer." She let out a tired laugh and Al could hear her take a drink and the sound of a TV playing. Her voice grew quiet. "Jesus, Kid, thanks for not giving me a hard time about the divorce. It got ugly with Everett. He put the screws to me. He left me when he found out we were married. I'd never seen him so mad. It was real bad for a while and it took me a lot to get him back. A lot . . . I want you to know I still have your ring. I'm looking at it as we speak. It sure was sweet of you to give it to me. It must have set you back a penny. I'll pop it in the mail tomorrow. And my God, Kid, what was the point of us getting married, anyway? We both know I'm too old for you." Mona paused and took another drink. "Anyway, you're lucky you're still in Reno. Nashville's stuck-up bad. The women are awful, but the musicians sure can play. They're the best, better than anything we've ever seen, that's for sure. So I guess I have to be grateful Everett got me in the door. If only I was twenty years younger . . . You know, we recorded three of your tunes, but the producer decided against them. They're moving me away from old-sounding country to a more modern pop sound. Your tunes are so sad, anyway . . . And you should see me now. I look pretty good, but what a lot of god-damn work. Everett has me going to a dietitian and I can't eat anything good. I had my teeth capped, too. It's all so boring, all the work that goes into it. And you should see my hair. I've cut a lot of it off. All the singers here have big hair, so we're betting I'll stand out more with short . . . Pretty soon I'm on the road for six weeks. You'd love my band. They're so good. Real slick pros, the guitar player is unreal, I don't know how they get so good . . . Well, I'd like to keep talking, but I'm beat. I'm starting to find if I sleep at least nine hours a night I can hit the notes. And luckily no more four-set casino gigs for me." She let out another laugh. "Well, good luck to you, Kid. We sure had some fun, and you sure were a sweetheart. In your own way, you cut me deep, maybe the deepest. But I gotta run now. I was sup-posed to be somewhere an hour ago. I just wanted to call and clear the air, and now we have."

5

The storm passed and morning came. Al looked out the window to see the horse still standing in the middle of the road. Small puffs of steam came from its nostrils, and its thick winter coat had a film of frost and snow on it. Al heated a large pot with water, and when it neared boiling, he took a cupful, made instant coffee, doused it with sugar, and drank it. He put on his coveralls, boots, and ski cap and took the pot outside.

The porch thermostat read sixteen degrees. The water in the horse's bucket was frozen. Al broke out the ice and poured in the hot water. The horse moved back a step when he did, and its breathing quickened, but it did nothing else. Al went back inside and looked through his food: a half case of Campbell's condensed soup, two jars of instant coffee, a quarter bag of sugar, a nearly empty tub of margarine, a third of a bottle of hot sauce, a quarter bottle of maple syrup, and a package of spaghetti. He boiled more water and put in the package of pasta. When it was cooked, he strained it and dumped it in a stainless-steel mixing bowl with the rest of the margarine in the tub. He salted it, ate a few bites, and took the rest out to the horse.

"I'm sorry, it's all I have," he said. "I'm gonna get my car started and then I'll get help from Lonnie. He'll know what to do."

The four tires on the emerald-green 1982 Monte Carlo were low but held air. Al brushed snow off the car and got in. It had been nearly seven months since he had started it. On the passenger-side floor were three empty beer cans and a mouse nest built into a Burger King bag, and on the backseat was an acoustic guitar, its neck broken off from the body and held to it by strings. Al put the key in the ignition and turned it, but the battery was dead. No lights came on at all.

In the trunk was a wooden box with cans of fluids, a set of chains, and three spare batteries with notes that Lonnie had put on each one.

The Best—almost brand-new. Gerry's spare from the tractor.

All right—charged but it's old and the spare for the pickup.

No idea—just found it in the barn. Kept it on the charger for two days.

Al took the one marked best and carried it to the front of the car, set it down, and opened the hood. The engine had more mouse nests. He cleared them and grabbed a toolbox he kept on the floor of the backseat. With two crescent wrenches and a screwdriver he got the terminals off the dead battery and connected the new one.

In the wooden box he found a can of starting fluid with a piece of paper taped to it.

Take the air filter off and spray this shit in the carb and then try to start it. Repeat until the engine runs. The air filter is the big black thing in the center with the wing nut. If you're reading this you should kick the shit out of yourself for not starting your car regularly. And for Christ's sake why won't you just buy a four-wheeler like everyone else?

Lonnie

Al took the air filter off, sprayed starting fluid into the carburetor, and went back to the driver's seat. The engine turned over fourteen times before the battery gave out. He put in the second battery, sprayed more starting fluid in the carb, and again turned the ignition. This time black smoke spewed from the exhaust pipe and the engine coughed a half-dozen times before it quit and the second battery gave out. The last one held no charge at all.

The Monte Carlo wasn't going to start.

Al sat in the front seat for a long time and didn't move. His breath fogged the windows; he cursed himself and thought of the broken guitar. He slumped down in the seat and closed his eyes.

It had been early fall when he'd driven in from the claim for groceries and seen a flyer for Tall Tom and the Tapaderos playing at the Tonopah Station in three weeks' time. He'd put the flyer in his pocket, and when the night of the gig came, he decided to go. He shaved, gave himself a sponge bath, and washed and greased back his hair. In his car he hung a dry-cleaned custom black suit and gray western shirt. His acoustic guitar and a notebook he put in the backseat. On the floor next to him were his shined boots and his dress belt and buckle. He wore the two rings and his Rolex wristwatch.

The plan was to buy groceries, see the show, and drive home. At Raley's he got a case of beer, a fifth of tequila, and a month's worth of dry and canned food. But by the time he passed the meat aisle he was starving and, without thinking, began throwing in steaks, bacon, and chicken. In the parking lot he put them on ice in the cooler he kept in the trunk and drove to the Banc Club. He carried his suit bag into the single-room casino, ordered a beer and a Hornitos. He drank the tequila and took the beer and the suit to the bathroom and changed.

Al knew Tall Tom and the Tapaderos and their pedal steel player, Bobby Winkle, from a time he had filled in as the guitar player for a Carson City group called the Saddle Brothers. It was 1988 and he was forty-three years old. The Saddle Brothers had a one-night gig at a rodeo in Corning, California. They played the after-rodeo party and Tall Tom and the Tapaderos played the evening dance. When both gigs finished, the two bands met at a bar and Bobby and Al became friends and, later on that night, set up gear in Al's motel room and played. After that, any time Tall Tom came through Reno or Lake Tahoe or Carson City, Al and Bobby would try and get together.

The lounge at the Tonopah Station had only seven people in it. Al walked in to see the years had taken their toll on the band. No longer did they have a lead guitar player, and the rhythm section was younger, kids in their twenties. The drummer wore shorts and a black tank top. He had a sleeve of tattoos on each arm and a shaved head. The bass player's arms were also covered in tattoos, and he had long blond hair and wore shorts and a San Francisco Giants jersey. The singer and rhythm guitarist, Tall Tom, was in his late sixties and six feet five inches tall and looked unwell. He had become overweight and his face had a gray and yellow tint. His white Nudie suit coat was stained, and a third of the embroidery was missing from the left sleeve. On his feet were dirty white tennis shoes, and black sweatpants hung low on his waist. When he bent over to change the settings on his amp, the few people there could see the crack of his ass. Bobby was to the right of Tom and in his mid-sixties with dyed brown hair. He had also gained weight but looked better in his turquoise-and-red-embroidered white Nudie suit and black ostrich-skin cowboy boots.

When the first set ended, Al said hello to Bobby, and the steel player did seem happy to see him. "Goddamn, Al," he said. "I was wondering what happened to you. It's been something like six years, and now I find you here? How the hell did you end up in a shithole like this?"

At the casino bar they had a drink. Al told him he lived on a ranch with a swimming pool two hours north of Tonopah with a woman who took care of him. A woman who had family money. He told Bobby he had seen the Tall Tom flyer taped to a mini-mart window and decided to drive down and see the show. They finished the drink, Bobby went back to work, and Al stayed careful. He drank only beer until the band finished their last set two hours later. Bobby put his gear away and Al went to the Monte Carlo. He took out his guitar, a bottle of Centenario tequila, the spiral notebook, and went to Bobby's room.

The band's drummer was Bobby's roommate. He sat on top of his bed wearing headphones, playing a video game on his laptop. A small practice amp was in the corner by the door, and a lap steel sat on the dresser. Bobby had a bucket of ice and brought out a cooler of beer from the bathroom.

The two men sat at a table near the window and caught up. Tall Tom's son was the bass player and was three weeks out of rehab for heroin and methamphetamine and Tom thought he should keep an eye on him so they were rooming together. A few months earlier they'd lost their fourth rhythm section in six years, and Tom's son and his friend were filling in. But the days of constant touring were coming to an end. The gigs were harder to get and Tom had diabetes and problems with his feet. He couldn't stand for four sets, but sitting was worse on his back.

"The money's shit, too. I've been making the same for fifteen years," Bobby said. "I've applied for a few straight jobs, but I just can't see myself being home every night. My neighbor's working for Albertsons. I think I'd go nuts, but he told me they're hiring and he'd put in a good word for me. I might have to do that. I just don't know . . ." He finished his beer and then opened the cooler and took out another one.

"Are you guys looking for any original songs?"

Bobby laughed and shook his head. "Shit, man, you ask that every time I see you, and every time I tell you the same thing. We haven't recorded anything in over twenty years. But let's get down to it. I want to hear your new ones before I get too tight."

Al opened his notebook and started: "Halfway Between Her and You," "The Bottle's the Only Friend I Got Left," "Lynette," "A Girl on the Streets of Tucson," "The Prison Bus," "A Busted Windshield and a Broken Hand," "Jim and I Set Out for Los Angeles," "The Woman Who Is Always in Love with Someone New," "The Boxer in Wichita," "The Man with a Thousand Scars," "The Bank Heist," "My Nerves Were Shot Then," "Waiting on a Winnemucca Bus."

It was still dark out when he left. He remembered that the neon sign on top of the Mizpah Hotel was lit. And he remembered standing in the parking lot when Bobby told him the songs he had played were some of the best he'd heard in a long time. He was almost certain Bobby had said it like that and that he'd kept straight the story of his life on a ranch with a woman.

But after that everything went blank.

He didn't remember falling and scraping his hands or the sound of the guitar breaking. He remembered only waking up in his car outside the Banc Club covered in vomit, his guitar in pieces, and his notebook gone. For over forty years of drinking, he'd seldom blacked out, but now he frequently did. The clothes he'd driven into town wearing were in the trunk and he put them on in the parking lot. It was dawn and there was no one on the street. He felt all right until he bent down to put his boots back on and knew then his bowels were about to go. His mouth began to water and he broke into a cold sweat. He was going to be sick at both ends.

He drove half a mile to the Clown Motel and decided to get a room and use the toilet and take a shower. He took the six hundred dollars of emergency money he kept hidden in a map in the glove box and walked to the lobby to find he had woken up the clerk. The man had to turn on the computer, and the computer was old and took time to boot.

Al tried to slow his breathing, but he was sick and sweat leaked down the sides of his face. The clerk got the computer to work. He took Al's money, gave him a room key, and Al left the lobby. But as he opened the door to the room, with relief finally in sight, his bowels let go. He was sixty-four years old and had shat himself in the doorway of a third-rate motel room.

In the bathroom he took off his clothes and threw up in the sink. He showered and, as he did, washed his soiled pants and underwear. He dried himself, wrung out his things, hung them on the shower curtain rod, and collapsed into bed. He woke five hours later, dressed, and left to look for the lost notebook. Up and down street after Tonopah street he searched, but the notebook and the songs inside it were gone.

He ate at Burger King and went back to his room. That first night he woke at three a.m. Regret and guilt, shame and sadness, ran in a circle that wouldn't stop. He curled in a ball and fell in and out of troubled sleep. When morning came, he dressed in his now dry clothes and again looked for the notebook. He got takeout from El Marques Mexican restaurant and watched an *Indiana Jones* marathon and slept for ten hours. He woke the third day feeling better. He watched *Rollerball* with James Caan. He again got takeout from El Marques and took a two-mile afternoon walk. He slept soundly again and on the fourth morning he went to A-Bar-L clothing store and bought a new shirt, a pair of pants, new underwear, and socks. He wore them when he checked out of the motel. At the Tonopah Station he ate breakfast and then went to the Main Street barbershop and had a haircut and a professional shave.

It was the best he had felt in months and he thought of renting an apartment in town. Living with running water, hot water, electricity, TV, and takeout food. He felt so good he stopped at the Clubhouse bar for a quick drink and left town drunk three hours later. When the pavement turned to gravel he stopped the Monte Carlo. He got out and opened the cooler to find the meat swimming in rancid water. When the smell hit him, he nearly threw up, but he found a warm beer inside, wiped the tainted water from it, and opened the can.

6

"You get as many women as everyone says, being in a band?"

Lonnie and Al sat outside the assayer's shack under the shade of a cottonwood tree. It was August, ninety degrees, and no clouds were in the sky.

"I guess you're around more women," Al said. "And a lot of the time the women are drunk or trying to party. Especially in the kind of bands I was in for a long time, where you play casinos or bars and you play all night."

"I wish I was in a band."

"You've just been out in the middle of nowhere for too long."

"Maybe, but I gotta say, being in a band sounds a hell of a lot better than working on Morton's ranch."

"I don't know, maybe," Al said. "What's going on with Gerry, anyway? He hasn't been by here in a long time."

Lonnie leaned back against the tree. He wore boots and jeans and a faded black T-shirt that read JT. "He won't see anybody now that he's selling his family's ranch. I think he's ashamed."

"What are you going to do when it's gone?"

"I'm not sure," Lonnie said. "But I know I'm going down to Globe, Arizona. His aunt lives there and I'm gonna drop off the horses he wants her to keep. After that, well, if he pays me what he owes me, I'm going to go on vacation. Maybe go to the Grand Canyon or maybe drive down to Mexico. I've never been there. What are you gonna do when I leave?"

Al shrugged.

"Man, I just don't understand why you live out here. You don't have electricity or even running water. And your car is a piece of shit and you never start it. It took me an hour to get it running this morning. And who's going to bring you food if your car doesn't start?"

"Don't worry about me."

"Yeah, you say that, but . . . You know, over the years you've hired me to do more and more shit. I do everything now. What are you gonna do when I'm gone?"

"I'll be all right."

"I don't know, man. I just don't get it. You say you got money, but you won't buy a four-wheeler or replace that fucked-up wood-stove. You give me a grand and I'll put a new one in. Or I'll get you a used motorcycle or at least a mountain bike, something in case you get in trouble. I'm serious."

"I know."

"But you won't."

"I will."

"When?"

Al shrugged. "Soon. I'm just in one of those phases where I can't pull the trigger on anything."

"Then at least start your car every few days and let it run for a half hour or so."

"I will."

"That motherfucker hates starting."

"I know."

"Well, I guess I've bitched at you enough," Lonnie said, and stood up. "I'm sorry, but it just seems crazy to me that you live out here the way you do . . . Anyway, I better get rolling. Morton has me cleaning out the barn."

Lonnie helped Al to his feet, and Al took three hundred dollars from his pants pocket and handed it to him.

"You always pay too much."

"I can't use a chain saw anymore. I'm too old to cut wood."

"And too lazy."

"And too lazy."

Lonnie put the money in his wallet. "Can I ask you another question?"

"Sure."

"What's it like being on a stage and having people go nuts for you?"

"Why you asking all this today?"

"I saw that movie Almost Famous last night. About the groupies and the bands flying around and playing concerts. It all seems so cool. And the girls, man, that one with the glasses . . ."

Al laughed. "I don't know about shit like that. For twenty years all I played were casinos. Those gigs, no one really ever cared, once in a while maybe, but not really. After that I just played bars."

"So it wasn't like that movie?"

"Not for me."

"Then why did you do it?"

"I don't know . . . I guess when casino bands were popular, I made good money and I got to play guitar for a living and I've always loved playing guitar. I only worked three or four hours a night and for a long time the money was consistent. There were a lot of gigs. After those dried up, I don't know . . . I like writing songs and for a while I got in a couple good bands . . . I guess there's something about being in a band, even a casino band, when it's good it feels . . . I don't know, I guess it's like being on a team. It just feels good when everyone is working together and you're doing a song you like. The noise of it, the sound, feels good, too. It gets inside you and maybe, in a way, you get inside it. You can just sorta disappear from everything, and at the end if people are clapping, well, that's a plus."

"*And then the chicks come?*"

"*Maybe . . . But not like you're thinking. You're thinking of rock stars. I was a thousand miles from that. I don't know anything about that. The kind of women . . . Well . . . Once I was in this band and we were playing in Boise. We stayed in a motel next to these three women who had just gotten out of prison. It was their first night being free. They were young and wild. Really rough. That's the sort of women you meet when you're in a small-time band.*"

"*I want to meet women like that.*"

"*No, you don't.*"

"*What band was that?*"

"*We were called The Sanchez Brothers. Two brothers were the singers, they played bass and guitar and they were really good, and the drummer was good, and we were doing my tunes. Jesus, that felt . . . It was the best band I was ever in.*"

"*Did you hook up with the prison chicks?*"

"*Nah, I was in my forties by then,*" Al said. "*I knew better. But the guys in the band did. There were four of us sharing one room. So I just went to the lobby, got my own room that night, and watched TV.*"

"*You watched TV over prison chicks?*"

"*Yeah, but* The Getaway *with Steve McQueen and Ali MacGraw was on and I had the whole room to myself. I was two blocks from a diner I liked and we were heading back to Reno the next day. The tour was over. For me, where I was at in my life, I'd hit the lottery.*"

Al woke up and thought of Lonnie, but he hadn't seen Lonnie in months and had no idea if he was even in Nevada anymore. He fumbled for the door handle and got out of the Monte Carlo. He sat on the ground ten yards from the horse. His hands were covered in dirt and grease and smelled of starting fluid. A blind horse in a high desert winter. A blind horse that licked snow but wouldn't drink the water he had set down or touch the spaghetti he'd left. Why did the horse have to stop in front of the assayer's office in the first place? And why was the horse alone, and how did it get there if it was blind? And what was he going to do if it didn't leave? And why hadn't he ever listened to Lonnie and just started his car?

Al's nerves gave out and he lay on his back in the snow. Above him, two contrails faded into a blue sky that seemed to go on forever. He closed his eyes and again dozed off. When he opened them, a Cooper's hawk was above him, floating on updrafts in the fading afternoon light.

Inside he heated a can of Campbell's condensed fiesta nacho cheese soup and sat in the recliner. An idea came to him and he quit eating. He found a plastic garbage bag and a pair of scissors. He grabbed a water bottle, put on his ski cap, and left. Up through the snow-covered canyon he went past the mine buildings and the last remnants of the old miner shacks. Two miles away and up three thousand feet in elevation to a place his uncle Mel called "the Big Bowl," a twenty-acre-wide meadow, now covered in snow, surrounded on three sides by mountains that rose to eleven thousand feet.

Al's legs shook, and he was so exhausted when he came to the meadow's edge that he lay down in the road, in the snow, and closed his eyes. He woke up a half hour later, his body stiff and cold, and got to work. He brushed snow off frozen meadow grass, cut it with the scissors, and put the clippings in the garbage bag. He didn't stop for two hours, and the bag was half full by then.

It was dusk when he made it back to the mine and the horse standing in the middle of the road. He dumped the grass by its front hooves and made four trips to stock the woodbin. He stayed inside and started a fire. By then he was so exhausted he couldn't even reach down to take off his boots. He just collapsed into his chair.

At three a.m. he woke, and he woke in a fit of panic, certain the horse was dead. He grabbed the flashlight and ran outside to see nothing had changed. The horse stood in the same place, its head down near the ground, its lower lip hanging out in sleep, the water frozen, the spaghetti frozen, and the grass untouched.

Inside he lit the lantern and took off his boots and his thermal coveralls and put on his sweats. He added wood to the stove, made instant coffee, and sat in the recliner and stared out the window into the blackness of night. A spiral notebook sat on the floor next to the chair. He flipped through the pages and stopped at a nearly finished tune called "The Killing of a Las Vegas Diamond." On the top left corner of the page he'd written ROLEX OYSTER PERPETUAL in large block letters and 1974–76??? Underneath that he'd written REX WINCHESTER.

Al was twenty-eight years old and the casino band he had been in for three years, the Ronnie Willis Band, a country covers group, had disbanded. Ronnie, the lead singer, had a breakdown in the middle of a set at the Gold Dust West and began yelling at the customers and staff and had to be taken from the stage by security. The next day he told the band he was done with music and moved back to Carson City to live with his mother. Al couldn't find another gig and had begun looking for a cooking job when he got a call from the manager of the

Wagonettes, a touring country-swing act out of Dallas, Texas. Their guitar player had been stabbed outside the Playhouse Lounge in Sparks and was in critical condition. The band had three weeks left in a residency at John Ascuaga's Nugget and needed a fill-in guitar player.

Al auditioned, got the job, and had a series of practice sessions with the band's pedal steel player, a man named Billy Mc-Clean. It was McClean who introduced Al to a musician he'd recently met named Rex Dembow, a struggling country singer who played under the name of Rex Winchester. Rex, handsome and rugged and thirty-two years old, had a voice that was a near match for Merle Haggard. He had recently left Las Vegas, where he had performed for ten years minus two stints in prison for identity theft, and now lived in Reno.

After a Wagonettes gig one night, Rex and Al sat together in a Nugget Casino lounge. Rex drank rum and Cokes and chain-smoked unfiltered Old Gold cigarettes. "To tell you the truth, Black Sabbath and Led Zeppelin are my bands. You can take all this country shit and throw it in the middle of a lake and blow it to hell for all I care. But the thing is, I can sing it. I mean I can sing rock, but it just don't sound right. No one thinks it does, but then I do a Merle tune and everyone thinks I'm Merle. Why I'm saying all this is that I know who you are and I want you to join my band and write songs for me. I got a booking agent and a good rhythm section. And once we get rolling, we can get us a steel player like Billy. And I want you to know one other thing before you say yes or no, I don't want to be Merle Junior anymore. That's what people call me. I been playing shitholes for years and everyone in every Podunk bar calls me Little Merle or Merle Lite. That ain't a bad thing, but it ain't my thing, you know? That's why I've been smoking so much. I'm hoping it'll get me some gravel. So you gotta write me songs that are different than Merle's. Way fucking different, but all in that same bullshit country world. You know what I mean? I want old-school but new and different."

Al nodded but kept silent.

"How long will you be playing with these guys?"

"Probably another month or two. Just depends when their guitar player gets back."

"The guy that got stabbed?"

Al nodded.

"Can you write me some songs by then?"

Al shook his head. "I don't think so."

"I know you ain't heard of me," Rex said. "So why would you trust me, huh? I mean I don't blame you. Let me sing you a song so you can at least hear me. Hear how good I am. It's a Merle tune called 'Skid Row.'" Rex stood up, took off his cowboy hat, set it on the bar, and sang the song from start to finish, his eyes never leaving Al. The people around them watched, and a passing cocktail waitress sat on a stool and listened. When Rex finished, they all clapped, then he put on his hat again and sat back down.

"You're a good singer," Al said. "And you're right. You sound a lot like Merle Haggard."

"So will you do it?"

"I could try. Maybe we play together a few times and I'll see if that gets me thinking about what kind of songs to write."

Rex shook his head. "Nah, that won't work. I need a committed guitar man in my corner and a full-time songwriter working for me. I gotta hit it big and hit it fast. I'm getting old, and if I get too old, people won't give a shit . . . Look, my whole life there's only been two things I've ever known for sure. Which chick I want and that I'm meant to be famous. I got the first, but I got sidetracked for a few years on the second and now I'm running out of time. So come on, what do you say?"

"I have to make a living," Al said.

"So it's money? That's the thing, huh?"

Al shrugged.

Rex went to his coat pocket and pulled out a roll of money with a rubber band around it. He also took the cash from his wallet and the change from his pants pocket and counted it. "This is all the money I have, every goddamn cent to my name—$6,073.87—and I'm giving it to you because I'm a serious man and I want you to know I'm a serious man. Will you write me the songs or not?"

"I don't know," Al said. "What if you don't like the ones I write?"

"That's my problem."

"How many?"

"Six to start out with. A thousand a song but I get the rights. They'll be mine. I need people to think that I'm the songwriter. I'll get more respect that way, they'll pay more attention. Are you cool with that?"

Al looked at the money. "You're serious, a thousand dollars per song?"

Rex nodded.

Al stared at the money and put the six thousand dollars in his coat pocket, told Rex to keep the rest and that he'd try his best.

He played with the Wagonettes through their Reno contract and then toured with them through Montana, Wyoming, Utah, and Colorado. They played more gigs in Kansas and Missouri and finished with three weeks of crisscrossing Texas. In Dallas, at the final gig of the tour, the guitar player who had been stabbed came to listen. He walked with a cane but was better and said he would be back after the band's monthlong break was over. Al was given a going-away party, a bonus, and a plane ticket home.

Three days later Rex showed up at his apartment. It was two in the morning and he beat on the door until Al answered in his underwear.

"How did you find out where I live?" Al asked.

"I followed you home the night I gave you the six grand," Rex said. "I had to know where my money was."

Al let him inside and went to his bedroom and dressed. When he came out, he took two bottles of beer from the refrigerator and handed one to Rex. Rex took a drink from it and said, "Well, I got us some gigs. They ain't the best, but we gotta start somewhere. It's all truck stops and small-town casinos, but they pay all right. I hope to hell you can do it."

"I told you on the phone I could. It's on my calendar."

Rex took his hat off, ran his hands through his hair, and put it back on. "Christ, I didn't think you'd be gone with that band for so long."

"Me, neither."

"So what gives? You got my songs or not?"

"I got a few."

"Then let's get to work."

Al grabbed his guitar and the notebook of songs he'd written for Rex and sat at the kitchen table and sang them. "When the Clock Strikes Three and I'm Not Home"; "The Only Way I Know Is Down"; "At a Pay Phone in Baltimore"; "There's a

War Inside Me"; "Hard Times in Easy Town"; "I Hit It Big but
It Hit Back Bigger (Now I'm Hitchhiking Home)"; "The Casino
Robbery"; "The Big-time Swindle Shakedown"; "Loving Un-
der Red Lights"; "Rundown Raquel's Hiding in a Room at the
Riverside"; "Hard Living, Hard Drinking, Hard Times"; "The
Night Connie Came to Room 33."

Rex couldn't sit still while Al played the songs. He paced the
room and drank a half-dozen beers and smoked a half-dozen
Old Golds. When Al finished the last one, Rex said, "We're going to be fucking famous, man!" and hit the kitchen table so
hard it knocked over the empty beer bottles. "Goddamn, you
wrote me twelve hits instead of six!" He reached into his coat
pocket, took out a roll of money with a rubber band around it,
and counted out six thousand dollars. "That's for the rest of
them. Can you get me some paper? I'm gonna copy these lyrics
down and memorize them. I'll know them all by the first practice. I got a photographic memory. I can remember anything,
and that's the truth."

Al went to a kitchen drawer and came back with a new notebook and a pen. Rex sat at the kitchen table for the next hour,
copying lyrics. It was dawn when he set a piece of paper in
front of Al with the twelve song titles listed and below them
a note that read: *Rex Dembow wrote and owns everything about
these songs.*

Al signed the paper and Rex folded it, put it in his coat
pocket, and left.

With the money, Al bought his mother a new stove, refrigerator, and TV. She left for work one morning and came home
to find them installed. He bought a 1969 Gibson SG, two five-
hundred-dollar savings bonds, and a gray suit. At the time
he was seeing a cocktail waitress at the Nevada Club named

Cynthia Connelly. She was going through a divorce and in the process of moving to her sister's house in Oklahoma City. Al picked her up from work one evening and drove her to San Francisco. The next morning they flew to Kauai, where he had rented a bungalow on a lagoon for five days.

7

To the band's first practice Rex came dressed as a gentleman cowboy in a black Stetson, a black western suit, a forest-green western shirt, and a bolo tie. Under his arm was a full-length mirror. He leaned it against the washing machine in the basement of the drummer's house. He took off his coat and dress shirt and sang in a white tank top while staring at his reflection. Every third song he did twenty-five push-ups. He had the body of a boxer, knew the lyrics to Al's songs without looking at notes, and could sing for hours without strain. The rhythm section, two brothers named Hal and Ted Harrison, were pros, and as much as Al tried not to, he became hopeful about the project.

In the spring of 1974 they began a series of tours in a 1970 Ford Econoline van. Three weeks on, two weeks off. By November they had done four runs, none of which made money, but the people who saw Rex Winchester liked him. The band got along, and after each tour they were paid what Rex said they'd be paid. Where the money came from, no one knew or asked.

After eight months together Rex booked two days at a San Francisco recording studio. They cut four of Al's songs to make two singles, "Hard Living, Hard Drinking, Hard Times" and "When the Clock Strikes Three and I'm Not Home" being the A sides of each. Rex drove to radio stations throughout the West, trying to get the songs played and set up more tours. He hired a publicist to promote them and had an endless supply of energy, money, and optimism.

But two weeks before a run of gigs in the Southwest, Rex was arrested at The Cal Neva in Lake Tahoe and accused of robbing and beating a man in a hotel room. Rex was put in jail for eight days but released with no charges filed. He told the band it was a misunderstanding he didn't want to talk about, and they kept on. "Hard Living, Hard Drinking, Hard Times" was re-pressed four times and played on stations throughout Texas, California, Nevada, Montana, Arizona, Oregon, and Utah. The band did gigs in casinos and small-town grange halls, truck stops, Red Lion Lounges, and bars. Al learned that Rex took steroids to keep in shape, Benzedrine for energy, and when he carried a bottle of Jack Daniel's onstage with him each night it was filled with apple juice.

In El Paso after the last gig of a three-week run, the band had a party at their motel. Rex paid everyone, had Mexican food delivered, and they celebrated until three in the morning. The brothers then went back to their room, Al passed out, and Rex stayed up. He showered, shaved, and dressed. At six a.m. he shook Al awake.

"Sorry, man, but we gotta talk business. Can you do that?"

Al sat up and nodded.

"There's nothing but driving for the next three days, so I'm gonna fly home. You and the Harrisons drive the gear back, okay?"

"Okay."

"On the TV there's enough food, gas, and motel money to get you there. I'd go with you if I could, but I got too many irons in the fire . . . If shit doesn't go south and you see me in Reno, I want this back." Rex had an envelope in his hand and gave it to Al. "If something does happen, use this ten grand for new tunes."

"Ten grand?" Al said, and got out of bed.

"I'll have more soon. I just need enough so we can make a full-length record." Rex opened the curtain and looked outside to the parking lot. "Man, I gotta say, I didn't know how expensive it would be to run a touring band. And I'm sorry I woke you, I really am. I just got jumpy and wanted to give you the dough. But now that you're up, you mind driving me to the airport? I want to get out of here before the brothers wake up and ask me a bunch of questions I don't want to answer."

Al dressed and drove him to the drop-off zone at the El Paso airport. Rex took a silver wristwatch from his pants pocket and handed it to Al. "It's for writing me the songs like you said you would. No one ever does what they say they're gonna. Not ever. But you did, and I won't forget it."

The watch was a Rolex Oyster Perpetual. It had gold inlays and what seemed like a diamond above each hour. On the back was an inscription that had been crudely crossed out.

"You all right?"

"I'm all right," Rex said, and got out. "Like I said, I just get jumpy before big deals go down." He shut the door, knocked on the hood, and went inside.

Four days later he was arrested and jailed in Las Vegas for beating an old man inside a Stardust Casino hotel suite. A woman named Candice Winterson was also beaten. The old man confessed to her assault but said it was in self-defense. He told the police it was his understanding that Candice was his girlfriend. In actuality she had been part of a con to rob and extort him. The old man discovered Rex and Candice worked as a team and had stolen over eighty thousand dollars from him. Rex was put in jail and Candice spent three weeks in the hospital with a fractured skull. When the police interviewed her, she flipped on Rex and told the police Rex was her pimp, that he beat her and made her do the things she had done. No formal charges were filed against her, and because of his priors Rex was sentenced to five to seven years in Northern Nevada Correctional Center in Carson City.

It was a year later when Al visited the prison. He carried a spiral notebook and was led to a table in the dining area where he sat across from a now gaunt Rex.

"How much longer you really gonna be in here?"

Rex shrugged.

"You all right?"

"I'm all right enough," he said, but his hair was greasy and thinning, and his skin looked gray. He had dark circles under his eyes, and his cheeks and chin and neck had patches of rosacea. "Who you playing with now?"

"You ever heard of Ronnie Willis?"

"The obese guy?"

"Yeah, I've been playing in his band again." Al looked at the families and convicts and guards around them and whispered, "Did you really do all the stuff they said?"

Rex shook his head. "I just got sloppy," he whispered. "I just got stupid and sloppy. Anyway, you got my new songs yet?"

Al opened the notebook, read out the lyrics, and described the sort of music he was thinking about for each tune. "Carson City Breakdown," "Times Are Tight and Keep Getting Tighter," "Disappearing Darlene," "Why Can't I Ever Let Go of You?," "The Carney Life," "Cassie's on the Con Again," "My World Died in a Las Vegas Suite," "Wasted and Worn Out," "Send to Prisoner 13099," "Tell Me Mister Which Way to El Dorado?,"

"Ain't It About Time for You and Me to Get Back to Being Me and You?," "Lucky Lucy the Lanky Lady from Louisiana," "The Reckless Life Is the Only Life I Know," "I Reached for the Top Shelf and Ended Up in the Well," "Help Me Brother I'm Sinking Fast," "There Ain't Nothing Down the Highway but the Darkness of the Road."

"Some I wrote to cheer you up. Some are okay and a couple are pretty good."

"I like them all," Rex said, and for the first time he smiled. His gums were inflamed and there were traces of blood on his teeth. He turned to an empty page of the notebook, wrote the names of the songs, and tore out the paper.

Rex Dembow wrote and owns everything about these songs. Rex paid Al $10,000 for them.

Rex signed his name and Al signed his. Rex showed the paper to the guard and put it in his pocket and stood up to go. "That ten grand is yours now. Mail me copies with the chords on them. They got a guitar here and I want to learn them so I'll be ready when I get out."

Six months later Al received a postmarked prison letter from Rex.

Al,

I ain't ever told you shit about who I am. But I will now because I just found out that my old lady, Candice, was killed. She was shot in the back of the head in a parking lot outside a club in Vegas where she worked. The last mark she chose was an old man from Chicago but she didn't do her homework. Usually I did that part but I was too busy with the band. I really thought she'd done a background check, but of course she hadn't. Turned out he was connected, related somehow to mobsters in Chicago. You never met Candice but that was by design. I didn't want to mix the two things until she and I could get out of the life. You might have seen her though, she came to some of our gigs and she's the woman who's standing next to me in the kimono in those promo photos I took.

The main reason I'm writing is that I want you to know it wasn't her fault when she turned on me. That was always the plan. Women do less time, I had a record and she didn't, so why make it that she had to do any time at all? She was the best chick I ever met. It's hard being in here night after night knowing she's dead. What I can't stop thinking about is, she's just gone and I won't ever know where she's gone to. I just don't see how people move on from shit like that. I sure don't feel like I can. I gotta say, Al, the whole world makes me want to throw up. I don't see the point of anything really. I can't even blink my eyes without her coming across my mind and I think it's driving me crazy.

She and I had been together since we were thirteen. I called her my Las Vegas Diamond. We met when we were foster kids in Henderson. Some of the shit we've done would make your skin crawl. Anyway, I got one thing to ask. Will you write her a song? Most likely they'll get me like they got her. So we might be done playing together after all. We'll see. You been more than all right to me,

62

WILLY VLAUTIN

and I gotta thank you for that. Not a lot of people in this world ever have been.

Sincerely,
Rex

Al visited with five songs written out and tabbed on typing paper. "The Night Belongs to You"; "Even a Prison Cell Can't Tear Us Apart"; "Every Minute, Every Hour, Every Day, Every Year"; "The Las Vegas Blowup"; "I'll Find You Wherever You Are and We'll Be Together Again."

The Rex who sat across from him that time was only a shell of who he had been. He barely noticed the songs and said nothing about them. He told Al he'd been getting in fights. There were three guys who suddenly hated him and he wasn't sure why or what to do about it. For the last five minutes the two hardly spoke and then Rex just got up, left the songs on the table, and walked away.

8

The lantern ran out of fuel and the fire in the woodstove died and day came. Al slept until the sound of coyotes woke him, their yips echoing in a chorus off the canyon walls. In a panic he jumped up from the chair. Would they attack the horse? Could they? And what about mountain lions?

He ran outside to see the horse still in the same place. His heart raced so fast he nearly collapsed. In the snow he searched for coyote tracks but saw none and went back inside, restarted the fire, and boiled water for coffee. The afternoon passed and night came, he ate a can of condensed broccoli cheese soup, grabbed his headlamp, and left.

The section of mine his uncle had worked was a hundred yards up the road, a roughed-out hole that went two hundred feet horizontally into the side of the canyon wall. It was the width and height of a single-car garage. The shaft had been started by a private owner in 1952 and decommissioned in 1956 with a wheelless 1947 Ford Super Deluxe crammed into the hole and chain-link fencing put over the entrance. His uncle had taken down the fencing, pulled out the Ford, and begun the long process of rebuilding the support beams that kept the tunnel from collapsing.

Al went thirty feet inside the shaft and came to a gray metal ammunition box and opened it. He took out his uncle's Remington 7400 and a box of bullets and brought them back to the shack. He loaded the rifle, set it on his bed, and drank a cup

of coffee and then another and then another. He decided he'd
watch over the horse until it grew light.

As a boy, from ages seven to sixteen, Al spent three weeks each
summer at the mine with his great-uncle Mel, his mother's
youngest uncle. Mel also lived in Reno and would pick up Al
and drive him to the claim in his work truck. They slept in his
trailer and Mel taught Al to shoot guns, bird-hunt, and fish,
and showed him the basics of construction and mining. Over
the years he also taught Al how to drive a car, a motorcycle, a
tractor, and a backhoe, and taught him the rudimentary ability
to cook. But his great-uncle was a quiet man, aloof, and seldom
spoke except to explain something or to ask Al to do something. And there was no TV or even a radio in his trailer. It was
either the sound of work, later on the sound of Al practicing his
electric guitar with no amp, or the silence of the high desert.

During their weeks together Mel never got angry with Al, he
was never mean or even gruff, but there was no warmth to him,
either. No comforting or encouraging words were said, and
they touched only with a handshake when Al got into the truck
at the start of the trip and at the end when he was dropped off
in front of his mother's duplex. But his great-uncle had always
been there for him. Even later on when Al was a grown man
and went back time and time again to the claim, a failed drunk
trying to dry out.

In 1945 Mel came home from the army and bought a one-
bedroom house off California Avenue in Reno. He was thirty
years old, worked as a mechanic during the day and a bartender
at night, and after four years of eighteen-hour days had saved
enough money to buy a run-down service station on Keystone

Avenue. By thirty-five he was married—happily, he thought, until his wife left him unexpectedly seven years later. Mel came home from work one evening to find her and her things gone. He was so overwhelmed and so unsuspecting that even after reading the goodbye note she had left, he thought she might have been kidnapped and called the police.

He fell into a depression he couldn't articulate or control. To combat it, he worked more. Seven days a week from six in the morning until the station closed at eight. To avoid being home he ate dinner at the Pioneer Casino each night and began walking to and from work. Eventually he began buying a pint of bourbon on his way home. He drank it in his living room while listening to the radio and, years later, watching TV.

Mel was in his mid-fifties when the pint became a fifth. He had a drink in the morning before work and had a bottle in the shop that he poured into his coffee throughout the day. It caught him when he was sixty; his stomach and throat began to give out. His doctor told him he would be dead in a year if he didn't stop. So Mel called a realtor and began the process of selling the station, the property it was on, and his house.

When Mel was in his early forties, his next-door neighbor, a woman named Norma Shear, came to see him. Her husband, a Whittlesea taxi driver, had died of a heart attack at fifty-six, leaving Norma a widow at fifty-three. While clearing out his things, she found a deed to a five-hundred-acre parcel and mining claim in central Nevada, northeast of Tonopah. She asked Mel what he thought and he told her he'd check it out. When summer came, he took a week off work and drove the gas station's pickup truck to the mining claim and fell in love with the area. He developed more than a hundred photos from the trip and laid them out on Norma's kitchen table. She stood bent over, using bifocals to make out what she was seeing. She told him she'd rather live in hell than ever set foot there and sold Mel the property for two thousand dollars with the understanding that if he hit it big on any strike, she'd get twenty-five percent of the mine's profit.

Mel camped on the claim for twenty years: a week in the spring, three weeks in the summer, and a week in the fall. He hunted chukar and sage hen and fished the few surrounding mountain creeks. He read prospecting books and learned to mine. He poured a concrete pad for the trailer, built an outhouse, drilled for a well, and bought an adjoining parcel of five hundred acres.

He was sixty-one when he sold the gas station and his house on California Avenue. He left Reno in a new truck that towed a twenty-six-foot travel trailer. On the way out of town he stopped at the Reno Humane Society and picked out a mutt border collie pup he named Curly. He left a fairly wealthy man with a good stock portfolio, a month of provisions for himself and the dog, a case of Early Times bourbon, and four cases of beer. He and the dog lived in the trailer and Mel spent his days working the claim. At night he doled out less and less of the bourbon until he was drinking only a half pint and two beers a day. When he came to the last fifth and the remaining six-pack, he poured them out and was done with his drinking life.

The gun was on the bed and the night wore on and Al worried. If he didn't get help, the horse would die, and it could be days before it did. He could shoot the horse, but there was a good chance he would make a bad shot. If he hit the horse in the neck or stomach, he would have to hope his nerves held so he could finish it off. And even if he killed it with his first shot and caused it as little pain as possible, it would be there, stuck in front of the assayer's office, for what could be months. The coyotes and turkey vultures would arrive, and if it grew warm, which it sometimes did in the winter, the stink would come.

His breath quickened and his body tensed. Even though he was isolated in the middle of nowhere his nerves still caused him great pain. A cold sweat came and he fell into the panic that had plagued him for most of his life and at times nearly killed him. He collapsed in the recliner and stared out in the darkness.

It was a month after Mona had left for Nashville that Al woke up one morning and felt, from the moment he opened his eyes, as though someone were trying to push him out of an airplane from thirty thousand feet. He couldn't make sense of it. He was heartbroken over Mona, that was true, but he had started a full-time casino gig as the guitar player for the Ronnie Willis Band. He was making good money and he liked Ronnie Willis and Ronnie liked his songs. As he lay in bed that morning he was a bit hungover but he wasn't sick. It wasn't booze. The night before, he had played the gig, eaten a late-night dinner at the Nevada Club, and gone to bed. Nothing he'd done could explain waking up in complete terror and panic.

In the shower he looked his body over to see if there was something causing the pain. But nothing was different. He dressed and made coffee and realized he had felt the same before. A month after Vern's death he had woken in the middle of the night, out of breath and crying. But that panic feeling of missing his uncle had happened only a dozen times, each episode lasting under a half hour. It was like a nightmare that dissipated the longer he was awake. He'd had the feeling other times, too. Once when his mother and he were in her car, a semitruck veered into their lane and almost hit them head-on. For ten minutes afterward he could barely breathe. Another time when he and Vern were up near Verdi swimming in the Truckee, he got a river shoe caught in a fallen tree at the bottom of a deep pool. He was certain he was going to drown and began to squirm and panic, but the shoe came off and he escaped. But in those times his rattled nerves made sense and the feeling vanished as quickly as it came. This time it didn't.

People went crazy in their early twenties. He knew that. A year earlier a friend of his from high school called out of the blue and asked him to lunch at Fong's Chinese restaurant. Al hadn't seen him since the summer after graduation. The friend showed up disheveled and overweight. His clothes were dirty, his hair unwashed. He smelled like he'd pissed his pants, and his shoes had black electrical tape keeping them together. He carried a notebook that had poetry written in his own constructed language. The poetry had algebra equations and notes about Elizabeth Taylor's vagina. The kid began crying while they ate and told Al he felt like his body was being split in two every time he closed his eyes.

Al had never prayed but he prayed that morning in the shower. He prayed not to go crazy like his friend and he begged and prayed for the panic to go away. But the feeling didn't go away. It was there a day, a week, a month, a year, and then finally another year before it broke. And what caused it to break? He'd never been sure. It wasn't one thing that he could pinpoint. It just sort of fell away from him little by little. But every morning for two years when he opened his eyes he had trouble catching his breath and his mind raced and fell apart and always he was so tired and shattered he could barely get through the day. Someone pushing him out of a plane at thirty thousand feet. It was the only way he knew how to describe the feeling he had from the moment he woke until he collapsed into sleep at night.

He told no one what was happening to him and asked no one for help. He was afraid if he told one doctor, then that doctor would tell another and eventually he would be put in the state mental ward. The same ward that his friend ended up in six months after their lunch. So, instead, he medicated by drinking. Because when drunk he wasn't being pushed out of an airplane at thirty thousand feet. The plane and the falling and the panic and fear disappeared with each drink he had. So he stayed out all night and slept all day. And when afternoon came and he got up, the panic would get up, too, and by the time he walked to the Cal Neva or Miguels Mexican restaurant to eat, it would be a part of him again. It would stay with him while he ate, while he walked home, while he drank coffee and played guitar in his kitchen, and while he performed his evening gig.

After six months of it, he bought a pistol, a .357, and decided to kill himself. At least once a month he put the stainless-steel revolver on the kitchen table. He could pick it up and he could put the barrel in his mouth but he couldn't pull the trigger.

In the paper was a help-wanted ad for a breakfast cook at Fitzgeralds casino. He applied and got the job. He also kept his gig with Ronnie Willis. On gig nights he wouldn't get to bed until two a.m. He left for Fitzgeralds at five. When he got home from cooking, it was two in the afternoon and he would be so exhausted he'd fall asleep until he had to get up for his evening gig. His hope was that the constant work would distract him, that it would derail the spiral he was in. He lost weight and got drunk seven nights a week. He destroyed his life in hopes of saving it.

The day he turned twenty-three he had a birthday dinner with his mother at her duplex. Afterward, on the way home to his apartment, he bought a six-pack of Coors. He drank the beers in his kitchen while he worked on a song called "They're Fighting Again Next Door" about the couple who lived below him. It didn't seem like a big deal at the time, bringing home a six-pack of beer, but in hindsight he supposed it was. As a kid he had made a pact with his mother that he would never drink, and when he broke that pact he made another with himself that he would never bring alcohol into his home. But that night, as he played guitar and drank beer in the safety of his kitchen, his loneliness and sadness over Mona, his failing mental state, and the uncertainty of his life as a musician disappeared. He worked on the song and drank and thought of nothing else. His apartment, which had become a sort of prison he struggled to get out of and hated to go into, became a haven.

9

Two coyotes appeared at dawn, trotting up a gully to the road and the horse. Al jumped up from the recliner and grabbed the rifle off the bed. His hands shook as he walked down the porch steps and waved the gun and screamed as loud as he could. The coyotes ran back down the gulley and disappeared. After that Al stayed outside. He broke the ice out of the bucket and added fresh water. He moved the grass closer to the horse's feet. He watched and waited and the day went on. When he grew too cold, he went back inside. He ate and sat in the recliner and watched.

At dusk the coyotes returned.

One was the size of a large dog and the other was smaller and had a slight limp. Al grabbed his uncle's rifle and opened the door to see the bigger of the two run at the horse and bite it on the back of its left hind leg. The horse kicked but was too slow. Al ran to the porch steps and again screamed and waved his arms, but this time the coyotes didn't leave. This time they weren't scared. The larger went at the horse's leg again. Al moved down the steps to the edge of the road but couldn't pull the trigger without the possibility of shooting the horse. So he aimed where the smaller coyote with the limp paced back and forth on a sagebrush hill.

He didn't want to kill it. He only wanted the bullet to land close enough to frighten it. But he hadn't fired a rifle in years and the shot echoed through the canyon and he stumbled back from the kick and the small coyote with the limp fell. The large coyote disappeared down the gully and the smaller one struggled to stand. The bullet had ripped the bottom third of its left front leg off.

Al walked twenty feet from it. He put another bullet in the chamber, pointed the rifle at the coyote's head, and fired. But again he missed and the bullet went into the coyote's stomach. It fell to the snow and blood pooled as it tried to get up. Al put another bullet in the chamber, walked three feet from it, and shot the coyote in the head and it was over.

Behind him the horse's breathing was worried. It hadn't moved more than a handful of steps and its back left leg now leaked blood onto the snow. Al waited and watched for the other coyote to return and night came and finally he went back inside. He laid the rifle on his bed and made coffee. He sat in the recliner and stared out the window and tried to stay awake, but he couldn't. It was three a.m. when he woke. He opened his eyes, so worried that he forgot to put on his boots. He ran outside in his socks to find the horse still there, standing under a cloudless, star-filled sky.

He put wood in the stove, changed his socks, and made more coffee. As he drank a cup and then another he knew there was no good outcome for the horse. The only answer was death. He would have to shoot it. He would have to put the horse out of its misery because, if he didn't, the coyotes would get it or eventually a mountain lion would find it. And even if that didn't happen, the horse wouldn't drink or eat, and the slow agony of that had to be worse than the momentary pain of a bullet.

It was four in the morning when he again put on his headlamp and walked back to the mine. He went past the gray metal ammunition box and stacks of pressure-treated six-bysixes and four-by-fours, past two battered wheelbarrows and a handmade wooden cart. It was a hundred feet farther into the mountain that he came to an olive-green metal chest. Inside, wrapped in a towel, were two bottles of Centenario Añejo tequila. On top of them, wrapped in a red shop towel, was the loaded stainless-steel .357 pistol he'd bought when he was twenty-two. On the handle was an aged paper note held by a dried-out rubber band.

Leave the pistol. The feeling will pass. I know you always forget this, but the pain will go away and you'll be all right. Get drunk if you have to but leave the gun. At least wait a day or two before you come back for it.

Al took one of the bottles and headed back out. An instant relief came. He would get to drink. Because to shoot the horse he would have to be drunk. There was no other way he could do it. He decided he would dole out the tequila in hour intervals to keep his head straight until dawn. Tight enough to have guts but straight enough to shoot the horse. He walked back to the office carrying the bottle, and the guilt of it rushed over him and he thought of his mother.

He was thirty years old when she had sudden back pain. She had trouble getting out of bed in the morning and trouble sitting at her desk at work. One day on lunch break she struggled to get up from the breakroom table and called Al. He picked her up from work and drove her to her doctor. She was admitted to St. Mary's Hospital, where she was diagnosed with advanced pancreatic cancer.

Each day after, Al sat with her in the hospital room. She seldom spoke except to tell him the things he needed to know. Her cash savings were hidden in three empty orange juice cans in the freezer. The titles to her car and the duplex were in her sock drawer as well as two dozen savings bonds. She explained which jewelry was worth money and where she thought he should sell it. She signed over the title to her car, signed over the duplex, and gave him power of attorney over her bank accounts. When she grew so ill she could barely speak, she gave Al a green felt bookmarker that held her Pioneer Total Abstinence Association of the Sacred Heart pin. A pin that represented a society held together by a belief in abstaining from alcohol: a white shield with a red heart inside it and, on top of the heart, a cross. She set it in Al's palm and wrapped her hands around his.

"I know you got the sickness," she whispered.

"I do."

"I should have never let you around Vern. I hate him for ruining you."

"It wasn't Vern's fault."

"Then I should have never let you have that guitar."

"It's not the guitar's fault," Al whispered.

"Then it's Mel."

"It's not Mel, either. It's my fault."

Her weepy bloodshot eyes stayed on him and her voice grew even more faint. "God makes mothers love their children, and I do love you, Al, but the way you live and who you've become has broken my heart more than I thought it could ever be broken."

"I know," he whispered. "I've always known that. I'm sorry."

Tears streamed down his mother's cheeks.

"Can I ask you a question?"

She nodded.

"Why have you always been so . . . hard. Cold to me. Is it you or has it always been me?"

His mother closed her eyes.

"And who is my father? You owe me that, don't you? I just don't understand why you haven't ever told me. Why do you always make me beg?"

But his mother didn't answer. She just turned her head and waved him away. They never spoke again except when she would ask him to turn the TV on or off or when she needed water or a nurse. When she died, Al moved out of his apartment and back into the duplex. He sold her furniture and bed and gave away her clothes. A man three houses down was a housepainter, and Al hired him to paint the interior. He had new floors put in the bathroom and kitchen and had the kitchen counter done. All of it was to erase the memory of the place. Erase the fact that he was thirty, living in his mother's home, and had become the thing she hated and feared most, an alcoholic.

10

An old casino highball glass sat on the table. Al drew a horizontal line halfway up it with a black marker. He opened the bottle and poured tequila to the line. A windup kitchen timer sat on the counter by the sink. He set it for an hour. One drink per hour. At first he didn't touch it, he only heated water on the stove and took the pot out to the horse and poured it into the bucket. He restocked the woodbin and made coffee and drank it in the recliner and looked out the window into the darkness and waited. He tried his best not to look at the timer, but he couldn't help himself. Fifteen minutes left. If he had the drink now, he could refill the glass and have another drink in just fifteen minutes. He'd have to wait an hour after that, but he'd worry about that then. He stared at it, got up, walked to the table, and sat.

He tried to take short sips but finished the drink in two swallows. The relief that alcohol had always given him was still there. Bad nerves to no nerves in one drink. There had been times when he first came to live at the mine that he'd get drunk and wild in the middle of the night. He'd get into the Monte Carlo and drive four hours to Las Vegas and rent a room for a week. A bender followed by a long recovery in a hotel room. He'd come home sober with a fresh haircut, a professional shave, new clothes, groceries, and always bottles of Centenario tequila and cases of beer. But those trips had become less frequent the longer he had lived at the mine. The isolation had begun to affect him. It made him uncomfortable around people. By the third year he struggled just to drive into Tonopah and get groceries.

He looked at his right hand holding the glass and saw the faded five-inch vertical scar on his wrist. A suicide scar was what people thought. But it wasn't. It was a scar of luck. The year it happened, he was thirty-two and surviving as a guitar player for a local Johnny Cash tribute band called A Boy Named Sue. It was because of that gig he was introduced to Lacy and Lynda Durrell, a country sister act in their mid-twenties who went by the stage name Lynda & Lacy. The band was looking for a guitarist, they invited Al to audition, and he was hired.

Lynda & Lacy played the casino circuit of Lake Tahoe, Reno, and Las Vegas. The songs were all covers, but slowly they incorporated a few of his songs and the money was good. Al got his own room and food vouchers, and the sisters could sing. They had a decent rhythm section, a good keyboard player, and the band got along. For the first eight months with Lynda & Lacy Al played 187 gigs of five sets a night before the band took a monthlong holiday break.

During his time off Al found a woman to make curtains for the duplex and bought a new couch and a 1974 sunburst Les Paul. He had nearly twenty thousand dollars in the bank and began shopping for a motorcycle that he could drive down to the claim in the summer and visit Mel. When his first Friday night off came, he wore his best suit and took a cab to the Halfway Club, an Italian restaurant on Fourth Street. He ate dinner by himself at the bar. It was midnight and he was half drunk when he decided to walk the three miles home. He passed motels and trailer parks, warehouses and auto repair shops. He came to the edge of downtown and was passing the Last Dollar Saloon when he slipped on a patch of black ice and fell on the sidewalk. When he stood, his hand was bent sideways and he stumbled a half mile to St. Mary's Hospital to find he'd broken his wrist in three places.

A surgeon put a five-inch metal rod from his wrist halfway to his elbow; the cast went from his thumb to his shoulder. For a month Al couldn't move or feel his fingers and was forced to quit Lynda & Lacy. The band hired a new guitar player and headed for Las Vegas and Al was left in a painkiller fog watching TV, listening to records, and at night, if he felt up to it, walking to the Pioneer Casino to eat dinner. When the pain had subsided enough he began taking meandering daytime walks through the city. He found an Italian restaurant he'd never seen called Franco's, and it was there, with his large cast resting on a booth table, that he met a twenty-nine-year-old waitress named Maxine Miller.

"Boy, just looking at your cast makes my arm hurt" was the first thing she said to him. Maxine had hazel eyes and red hair that came to her shoulders, and her skin was freckled and pale. She was dressed in black pants and a white collared shirt with a black apron tied around her waist. There was a sadness to her that Al felt from the moment he met her. It was like she lived her life with a slight limp, a brokenness she couldn't repair. She was beautiful to him because she was a bit beat-up and weary-looking. She had gallows humor and a face that said, *Maybe you win every single time, but you'll never get everything.*

Al began going to Franco's every other day for lunch. He'd sit in the back in the same booth, set his cast on the table, and Maxine, the only lunchtime waitress, would wait on him. It took him two weeks to ask her out, and when he did, she told him she was seeing someone and couldn't. But a month later she stopped at his table and said she'd broken up with her boyfriend and was now living with her mother.

They ate at the Mapes Casino on their first date and watched *The Deep* at a downtown movie theater. She stayed the night at the duplex. After that, they were always together. Al's cast came off, his wrist healed, he played pickup gigs and lived off his savings. They had dated less than three months when Maxine borrowed Al's car and moved her things out of her mother's apartment and into the duplex. Al knew their attraction lay in that they were both damaged, and that they could admit it, articulate it, and until then both had never met anyone else who could or would. And because of that, they worked. Because of that, she became the best friend he'd ever had.

Maxine had grown up in Winnemucca with her mother, father, and little brother. As early as she could remember, her father had punished her for the littlest things. If she knocked a glass over or ran in the house, he would spank her until her mother would force him to stop. The older she became and the more she looked like her mother, the worse the punishments became. There were arguments between her mother and father over it, her mother begging him to stop hurting her. So he began doing it only when he was alone with Maxine.

When she was fifteen her little brother had to go to Reno to have surgery to repair a hernia. Her mother and brother were gone for three days. It was the first time Maxine had spent the night alone with him in years. He was normal the first night, but the second night, when he came home from work, it began. He grabbed her by the hair while she was doing dishes. She screamed at him, "Fuck you," and he threw her against the refrigerator. He made her take off her clothes, lie flat on her stomach on his bed, and he spanked her until she begged him to stop.

She told no one what had happened, but a month later she stole her neighbor's Buick LeSabre and three thousand dollars her father kept hidden in a toolbox in their basement. She drove to New Orleans because she had just read *A Streetcar Named Desire* in school. She washed dishes at a restaurant in the French Quarter and lived in the car. After a month she moved in with the restaurant's thirty-three-year-old dinner shift bartender. She was with him two years, until he began locking her in their bedroom when he wasn't home. By then she was a waitress at the same restaurant. During her shift, her boyfriend would stand behind the bar and watch her. If she was too flirtatious with customers or other waiters, he would spend hours in their apartment interrogating her. He became violent. This went on until she stole his car, his coin collection, and everything else of his she thought she could get money for, and left the state.

The money ran out in Florida and she was caught shoplifting at a Winn-Dixie in Tampa. She was seventeen and living in her ex-boyfriend's car, which he had reported stolen. She was sent back to her mother, who was now single and living in Reno in a one-bedroom apartment with Maxine's brother. She enrolled in high school but dropped out after two months and went back to waitressing.

There were two other older men Maxine had lived with after that first one in New Orleans, but each relationship ended badly and nearly the same. Her boyfriends became controlling and eventually violent. Maxine struggled to keep jobs due to periodic spells of depression that became so paralyzing she couldn't get out of bed.

But with Al she didn't slide as often or as hard, and when she did, she was never cruel and never raged. She just disappeared a little here and a little there, and Al understood that, and regardless of where she was at, they got along.

On their days off they would stay in bed late and Maxine would get up and make afternoon meals. She called it "being on Al time" because he was so slow in the mornings. He would drink coffee and play her songs at the kitchen table and Maxine understood the darkness and saw the beauty in them. And she never gave Al a hard time when his nerves gave out or when he himself would stay in bed all day or get blind drunk for nights in a row. He was a good drunk then, too. Like his uncle Vern, he could be too sentimental and cry too easily, but those were things Maxine liked more than disliked. He was never violent or jealous and never said demeaning things to her. He never tried to control her.

Maxine didn't mind the rest. How Al spent too much money in bars or how he was often too hungover to do much of anything if he didn't have to. So much of his life back then was spent half sick, trying to recover from the night before, but then the three men Maxine had lived with previously were heavy drinkers. Her father and brother were also big drinkers. Al knew he was lucky in that she thought all men were that way because she had never been close to a man who wasn't.

They had lived together five months when Maxine came home from work and said, "I have a present for you." Al was sitting at the kitchen table. The Telecaster was in his lap and a spiral notebook sat open in front of him. "Can you take off for a week starting tonight?"

"Sure," he said. "Why?"

"We're going on vacation."

"Where?"

"You'll see, but we'll be gone five days and we gotta leave pretty soon."

She told him to pack a bag and bring his guitar, a swimsuit, and river shoes. In the trunk was her own suitcase, a cooler, and two sacks of groceries. Al loaded his things and Maxine drove them less than a mile to River House Motor Hotel, where she had reserved a deluxe suite for five nights.

The room was on the second floor and Chinese-themed, with white shag carpet and traditional landscape paintings of villages and forests and bridges on the walls. The light fixtures were faux paper lamps, the bedspread was white with Chinese writing on it, and the furniture was glossy black painted with bright flowers. The bathroom had both a tub and a walk-in shower large enough for two people. On the balcony were two chairs and a table that looked over the Truckee River. Al leaned against the railing and looked east, thirty yards down the river, to where he and Vern had gone swimming years before. He pointed to the hundred-year-old cottonwood tree that stood on the bank. "Did I ever tell you my uncle Vern and I used to hang out under that tree?"

"You told me," Maxine said, and leaned on the railing next to him.

"Did you get us the room here because of that?"

"Yeah."

Al went to her and kissed her and tears welled in his eyes and he told her he loved her. They went to bed with the balcony door open and the sound of the river rushing past. In the room they drank and fucked for two days and left only to eat. On the third day Maxine went back to her job at Franco's and Al stayed behind. When afternoon came, he walked to the restaurant and picked her up. On the way back he bought two bottles of Orange Crush and they changed into their swim-suits and swam in the same deep pool underneath the same cottonwood tree that he and Vern had twenty years before. On warm river rocks they sat and Maxine's hair was wet and she wore a blue bikini and Converse tennis shoes and sunglasses. She sat cross-legged and held the Orange Crush in her hand and looked out at the Mapes and Cal Neva casinos.

"Can I tell you something, Al?"

"Sure," he said.

"I just . . . I just want you to know that deep down I always knew I'd get lucky. That someday I wouldn't be alone. That I wouldn't always feel so alone. I didn't know when it would happen, but I knew somehow it would. I just never imagined it would take this long or that I'd . . . that I'd get so ruined along the way. That I'd get so hopeless. I remember when I was liv-ing in that car in Florida. Sometimes I'd just curl in a ball and say to myself, 'My lucky time will come. My lucky time will come.' I'd say it over and over. And I really tried to believe it. Believe that someday, somehow, a door would open a little bit and I'd be smart enough to walk through it, and once I did, I'd be different. I'd be . . . I haven't been great in life, Al. I've been with people and done things that make me so sad that I've just wanted to give up and die. I'm not playing around when I say that. I . . . But now . . ." She looked at him and smiled. "Now I'm nothing more than a part-time ledge walker."

"A ledge walker?"

"Just walking on the edge of things. Always one or two steps from jumping off. For the last few years, before I met you, I'd been walking that edge closer, you know?"

"Yeah."

"You do know, don't you?"

"I felt that way most of my life."

"That's why I'm telling you. Because you understand what it means to be so close to giving up that all it takes is one more step. But I'm not going to take that step. Because for me, the door I was talking about has finally opened and I'm not gonna stay scared or hate myself. I'm going to go through it because on the other side is you . . . I don't care if I'm making a mistake saying all this. Or if it causes you to run away. I'm just so tired of walking the ledge that I'm gonna give everything to you. Everything I have . . . Did I ever tell you about my uncle Sailor? He was a cowboy who worked a ranch outside of Elko."

"I don't think so. How did he get the name Sailor if he was a cowboy?"

Maxine wiped her eyes and took a drink of the Orange Crush. "When he was young, he went to San Francisco and got drunk with some sailors on shore leave. They all got tattoos, so he did, too. He got a big one of a woman on his forearm, a sailor pinup girl. He also got *HOLD* on his right knuckles and *FAST* on his left. I guess that means not to give up, not to ever let go of the rope. Everyone at home made fun of him because no one back there had tattoos. They began calling him Sailor and the name stuck . . . Years later, he broke his leg getting bucked off a horse, and he lived with us. He was my dad's little brother and he was maybe thirty and had a huge cast on his leg. All day long he just sat on our porch and sucked on lemon drop candies and listened to the radio. Sometimes I'd walk by and he'd be just sitting there so sad-looking. I don't know why he was so sad, but even as a kid I could feel it. I really could. In his own way I think he was a ledge walker. My mother said he was the loneliest man she'd ever met. When he healed, he went back to the ranch, but eight months later he had bad luck again. This time a horse kicked out when he was shoeing it and he broke three ribs. My dad gave him money so he would stay in a motel in Elko and not with us. It all seemed so hopeless for him . . . And then . . . And then he met a maid named Gladys. She cleaned his room and they fell in love. I'm serious. They did. They got married and . . . You know, they came and visited us a few times and they were really happy. They loved each other and . . . they . . . they got lucky, Al. He was saved because he walked through the door."

A jet flew overhead and left a long lazy contrail across the blue sky. Cars and trucks went across the Lake Street Bridge and the sun began to disappear behind the Sierras. Maxine put her feet in the river water and set her empty bottle on the rock.

"You know for years I've been getting more and more lost in my head. It's like swimming farther and farther out. Getting so alone and hopeless that I was almost certain there was no way I could ever get myself back. I don't know why I do it. I really don't. But I just wake up in the morning and keep swimming farther out. Do you know what I mean?"

"Yeah, I know," Al whispered.

"Ledge walking and swimming." She laughed and dropped into the river. Only her head stuck out of the water and she looked at him and smiled. "But you saved me from the sea, Al. You saved me from swimming so far out that I would never be able to get back . . . I know it's a gamble telling you all this. I've been waking up in the middle of the night worrying about telling you. About me ruining everything. But I'm tired of always losing things because I care about them. And Jesus, I'm tired of being scared. I just love you so much I had to tell you. I love you so much I can't help but tell you."

The last day at the River House, Al walked Maxine to work and afterward he went to Premier pawnshop on Virginia Street and bought her a gold wedding band. He bought a bottle of champagne from a liquor store and went to the duplex, put on his best suit, his best shirt, and boots, and walked back to Franco's and waited across the street until Maxine got off work. He gave her the ring outside the Mapes Casino in the fading warm afternoon light. They celebrated with a drink at the Sky Room and two hours later were married at the Park Wedding Chapel.

But thinking of Maxine was like a drink itself. Heaven and relief that soon disappeared into sickness and regret, sorrow and self-hatred. He looked out the window and the worry over the horse came back and the week at the River House and the songs he'd written for Maxine and their time together disappeared. "River House #3," "Saved from the Sea," "Waking Up in a Chinese Room," "Me and My Maxine," "Living in a Car in Florida," "The Ballad of Sailor & Gladys," "Drifting Out Past the Breakers," "Crown Royal and a King-Size Bed," "Maxine Don't Go Fading," "Our Clothes Were in a Pile on the Floor," "The Lost Week," "Sleeping by the River," "The Cottonwood Tree," "The Week Time Stopped," "Swimming Under Casino Lights," "A Girl Floating on a River," "I Can't See the Shore," "Hold Fast," "Walking That Ledge," "Maxine #6," "The Girl and the Bartender from New Orleans," "The Woman with a Scar That Never Healed," "I Didn't Know Where I Ended and Where You Began."

11

Dawn came and the horse hadn't moved from the road. In the stark light Al could see its ribs and noticed for the first time its swayed back. Its hind leg had stopped bleeding and only traces of blood were on the snow near it. The horse's head hung low, flecks of snow covered its mane, and again its lower lip hung out in sleep. The temperature was nine degrees.

The cooking timer rang. Al got up half drunk and went to the table and poured tequila to the marker on the glass. He drank it in three sips and knew if he was going to shoot the horse, the time to do it was then. Drunk but not too drunk. His mind was nearly blank. There was no fear or worry. The rifle was on the bed and he picked it up, put a bullet in the chamber, and went to the table and took a long pull from the bottle.

Outside was quiet and the sky cloudless. The horse was there in front of him. The mountains around them were bright with snow and below, the valley disappeared into white. He stopped five feet away. He could see the horse's swollen eye sockets, the brush hanging from the left eye, its thick winter coat, and the hard scars of its life printing out a history across its body.

"I'm sorry," he said. "I just don't know what else to do." Tears welled in his eyes and he raised the rifle. He pointed it to the horse's head and stood until his arms grew shaky and tired. He lowered the gun. Three times he tried to shoot it and three times he couldn't. He sat on the ground and stared at the horse. Its legs were covered in mazes of faded scars. Al took a handful of snow and put it in his mouth. Barbed wire was all he could think of, and thinking of the horse alone and in trouble, wrapped in barbed wire, was too hard to imagine.

He thought of the birth of the horse. The hope in that. The hope that it would be all right and live an all right life. That it would amount to something and live without too much pain. The hope that, at least for a time, it would have an easy run. That it would never end up blind in the middle of nowhere with no friends and no outcome other than death.

As he watched it, he knew then that he had most likely lost his mind. Because he felt that he and the horse were the same. And because of that the horse couldn't be real. His mind had finally betrayed him by bringing him the saddest thing he could imagine. His mind had brought the blind horse so Al would go mad and in that madness he'd be set free.

He watched the horse breathe, he watched it lick snow off the ground. He watched it sway as it stood and he didn't know anything anymore. It seemed real and if it was real then he needed to give it mercy. Because he himself needed mercy. He got back up and again pointed the rifle at the horse's head.

"Please," he whispered. "Please give me the strength to pull the trigger and let it be over." He stood until, again, his arms shook from the weight of the gun and finally he lowered it for the last time.

He couldn't shoot the horse.

He sat in the snow for a long time until he grew cold and went inside. He unloaded the rifle and took another pull from the bottle. He looked out the main window and saw a kestrel sitting on the porch railing, its orange and blue feathers and black barring. It was watching the horse. Al watching the kestrel watch the horse. When it flew off, Al heated a can of Campbell's chicken and stars soup and ate it while standing. He took another drink from the tequila bottle and decided he'd walk to the top of the canyon ridge in the faint hope that he could see down into the valley and that a car or truck would somehow be there and could help. In a backpack he put a water bottle, a can of soup, and a can opener and then left.

12

It was a mile to the ridge on a narrow snow-covered switch-back trail and he climbed fifteen hundred feet in elevation, his legs shaking and his heart pounding. He reached the top and sat on the ground exhausted and drunk and looked out over Big Smoky Valley. But he could find no hunter's camp or parked truck or car. There was no sign of humanity at all. Even the main gravel road was lost in the whiteness of snow. Above him a blue sky went on as far as he could see, and around him a freezing wind blew. For an hour he watched and waited but there was no change. There was nothing. He got to his feet unsteadily and headed back down. His stomach soured and he threw up the soup and the tequila into the snow. He kept walking but grew dizzy and again nauseated and he struggled not to fall. In the middle of the trail he sat and put a handful of snow in his mouth and closed his eyes. Lancaster, California, came to him and he thought of Lancaster only when he was fever-sick or depressed or when he wanted to wallow in his failures and punish himself for the drunk he had become.

It happened on the fifth night of a two-week run during a gig at Dino's Truck Stop Lounge on the outskirts of Lancaster, California. Al was fifty-seven and on his third tour with the Gold 'n Silver Gang when he collapsed mid-set. There were thirty people dancing and seventy-five people in the room.

The band stopped and carried him to the van. They went back in and continued on and Al vomited chicken-fried steak and gin and tonics over the bench seat and into an open box of CDs and T-shirts. When the band loaded out and saw what Al had done, they fired him. They drove him to a motel, paid his room for the night, put forty dollars in his shirt pocket, carried him and his gear inside, and left.

Al woke the next morning to a maid knocking on the door. He had the forty dollars, a suitcase, an amplifier, and two guitars. In his wallet was eleven dollars. He had no credit card and his guts were ruined and he spent the next half hour on the can. When he got out of the bathroom he collapsed into bed and again fell asleep. The manager knocked on the door and told him he had to pay for another night or check out. He gave the manager twenty dollars for an extra hour and stayed until the phone began ringing.

Across the street was a bar and he took what he could carry in one trip, the guitars and suitcase. He left his amp, a 1973 Fender Deluxe, in the room. He was so sick and his nerves so shot that he didn't even ask the motel staff to hold it for him or leave a note on it. He just left it.

The bar was called The Ninth Hole, and he drank until his thirty-one dollars ran out. The bartender told him of a pawn-shop four miles away, and in the afternoon heat Al left with his guitars and suitcase. He hadn't eaten and grew weak as he walked. He came to a park and sat in the shade of a California pepper tree. In his shaving kit he found a five-dollar bill and three dollars in quarters, and in his guitar case he found another fourteen dollars. At a mini-mart, he bought two forty-ounce beers and a burrito. A closed warehouse was at the end of the block and he sat under the loading dock awning and ate the burrito, drank one of the bottles of beer, and fell asleep. It was dusk when he woke and by the time he found the pawn-shop it was closed. He drank half of the last forty and slept on the ground. In the morning he finished the bottle and waited for the shop to open. When the lights turned on he went inside with the 1959 butterscotch-blond Telecaster guitar that Herb Marks had given him and a 1940 Martin D-28 acoustic.

The kid behind the counter said the owner was the one who knew guitars but that he was out of town. Even so Al took both out of their cases and set them on a long glass counter. The kid wore a Denver Broncos jersey. He chewed gum and barely looked at the guitars and said he would give Al a hundred dollars cash for each. Al tried to explain the kind of guitars they were, but again the kid told him he didn't know anything about guitars and that Al should come back the next day when the owner was working. There were bits of burrito on Al's shirt, he was dirty and sweating, his skin was gray. His breath was foul. He seemed like a bum, and the guitars, to someone who didn't know about guitars, seemed used up and worn out.

Al asked the kid to look up their value on the computer or call a guitar shop and tell them what he had. They were worth real money, he explained. They were expensive guitars. He told the kid he didn't need a whole lot of cash but he needed more than a hundred each. He was desperate, he told him. He was at the bottom, he said.

The kid refused.

Al began to lose his temper. "Come on," he said. "It's hard enough for me to sell them. Just look them up. Call any guitar shop and they'll tell you. Don't be a sack of shit. I swear to God they're worth a lot of money. You'll do good on them."

"Like I said the last three times, the owner handles guitars. All I can do is a hundred dollars each."

Al hit the glass case with his fist. "Come on man, just give me two-fifty each."

The kid became nervous. "I want you to leave," he said, "or I'll call the police."

More than anything, as Al stood there shaky and undone, he wanted it to be over. He was done with music, with writing songs that no one heard, with always playing nothing gigs in nowhere clubs for people who only wanted to talk and drink. And he was through waking up in the middle of the night to write down lines that came to him. He was done with stewing over songs until he was half mad. And no matter what he did or how hard he tried, his songs were good but never great. How many notebooks had he filled with half-good songs, songs that were almost? How many hours and months and years had he toiled and tinkered? And Jesus, how many hours had he spent learning cover songs he hated? And why did people always request such horrible songs? And why were the tunes he loved most never popular?

And he was through with sitting in vans day after day, worrying that the driver wasn't paying attention or would fall asleep or that they were driving too fast for the amount of weight they were carrying. Was the van too old? Were the tires too worn, the road too icy? Snow, wind, semis, bad drivers, driving in the middle of the night. The worse the band, the longer the drives. And new bands always wanted to drive at night.

If he looked back on it, how much of his life was spent just killing time? Waiting to load in, waiting for sound check, waiting for dinner, waiting for the gig to start, waiting to break down gear when the gig was done, waiting to load out, waiting for the band member who'd gone missing, waiting to get to the motel, waiting for the key to the room. If he added together the hours he'd spent writing tunes, waiting for gigs, getting to gigs, playing gigs, and also all the hours he'd spent drinking in bars or in bed hungover, what else had he done in his life?

"Come on man, please," Al cried. "I'm begging you."

The kid's voice was now shaking. "If you don't leave the store right now, I really am calling the cops."

"You're really gonna be that kind of motherfucker?" Al yelled.

The kid went to the back wall where a phone hung and began dialing a number.

Al looked at the acoustic guitar and thought of Lacy Durrell and a wave of rage and self-hatred came over him, to the point where he picked up the Martin off the counter and swung it down on the metal-edged glass. The old guitar exploded. The neck in his hands, the strings flapping about, and the body scattered on the unbroken glass counter and the floor. A four-thousand-dollar guitar broken into irreparable pieces. The kid picked up a baseball bat with his right hand and held the phone in his left.

Al walked down the street with the Telecaster and his suitcase. With the last of his money he bought two forty-ounce beers and sat under the same warehouse awning. The next day he stood outside a mini-mart and tried to sell the Telecaster. He was there for two hours when a man drove up in a pickup and looked at the guitar. The man could barely contain his excitement when he saw it.

"Why you selling it?" he asked.

"I'm broke."

"Just walking around with a guitar?"

"I got left by my band."

"Your band?"

"We were playing at Dino's Truck Stop."

The man nodded. "It's not stolen?"

"No," Al said.

"What do you want for it?"

"Two hundred and fifty."

"And you're sure it's not stolen?"

"It's not stolen . . . All I ask is if I get back on my feet and you want to sell it, you give me first chance to buy it."

"Sure," the man said. He looked around to see if anyone was with Al and then went to an ATM inside the mini-mart and came out with the money. Al took a black marker from the guitar case and had the man write his name and phone number on a piece of scrap paper. The man then gave Al the $250, took off the leather guitar strap that had *Al Ward, Reno, Nevada* stamped into it, and got into his truck with the guitar and left. Al put the money in his wallet, put the strap in his clothes bag, and bought a forty-ounce bottle of beer, an Oscar Mayer Lunchables, and a pint of tequila. He walked three blocks to a vacant lot behind an RV dealership and sat in the dirt under the shade of a willow tree.

For forty-three years he had lived with that Telecaster. He'd left it in cars, taxis, vans, motel rooms, and houses. It had been lost on flights, left on a Greyhound bus, and left at clubs. It had been stolen out of a bar in Reno only to show up a month later at a pawnshop on Virginia Street. Dozens of near misses and near catastrophes, but no matter how foolish Al had been, he and Herb Marks's Telecaster had always found each other again. Together they had been through thousands of gigs and endless hours of playing and practicing. Al had the pickups replaced once, refretted it three times, and bought four cases for it over the years. The guitar he'd brought to nearly every gig in his life was in the cab of an amateur blues player who bragged that he had more than thirty guitars at home. He had given his best friend of forty-three years to a guy who, on the bumper of his truck, had a sticker that read *A Blues Man Is the Only Man.*

There was a motel down the road called the Town House. He checked in that evening, took a shower, changed his clothes, and walked to Bob's Liquors and bought a fifth of Hornitos and a six-pack of Coors. He stayed for a week until the money ran out. After that he spent three nights at Grace Resources homeless shelter before calling his uncle Mel's lawyer in Tonopah, Carl Kennedy, who handled Mel's estate and was his emergency contact number. Al asked Carl to drive out to Mel and tell him that Al Ward was in bad shape and needed help.

Eight hours later Al picked up the homeless shelter's phone to hear Mel's voice. "Are you all right?" the old man asked.

"Not really," Al whispered.

"What's going on?"

Al was sitting in a small empty room next to the dining hall. Outside a dozen people were talking at a foldout table. He cleared his throat. "A while ago, six or seven months ago . . . I got home from a tour and there was a message on my phone from my ex-brother-in-law, Harold. He told me that Maxine had killed herself."

"Maxine?"

"Yeah."

"I'm sorry, Al. I'm so sorry to hear that."

"Yeah," Al said, and began to weep. "The thing is, when I hung up I felt . . . I felt so guilty . . . guilty like I'd done it to her myself. And maybe I did. But also I didn't, you know? I didn't.

But the guilt . . . The guilt just seemed to get more every day, not less. I couldn't stop thinking about it. My mind . . . It just got stuck there, Mel. It got . . . Maybe her dying was just an excuse for me to go off the rails, an excuse to give up. There's some truth to that. I've been struggling for a while. Just living but getting tired . . . I started another tour with this band called the Gold 'n Silver Gang. They're the shittiest band I was ever in. Maybe that's part of it, too. All those years playing only to end up in a bad country band with guys I didn't like."

"So you hit the bottle?"

"Yeah." Al wiped the tears from his face.

"And it turned on you?"

Al laughed. "Yeah . . . I started drinking before gigs. I started drinking in the mornings. Both of which I'd never done. I might be a fuckup but I never fucked up a gig. I never played drunk. I think I was just so . . . disgusted with myself, you know? I'd been limping along for so long that maybe I just wanted to get caught. And I did. I'm in Lancaster, California, at a homeless shelter and I called you because I'm a wreck and I don't know what to do. It's hard for me to ask for help, but I really need your help."

LEFT IN LANCASTER

My guts are ruined and my mind ain't clear
I've blown any chance I've had of getting out of here
I'm sick and lost and disappearing faster and faster
I'm drunk and broke and living on the skids in Lancaster

I got no one to blame and the wounds are self-inflicted
I try to live in gutters and sleep in ditches
I run from kindness and find comfort in grifters

I turn from any house and close my eyes to any pasture
I'm drunk and at the bottom and living on the streets of
    Lancaster

The ice is cracking, can't you see?
There are people nearby but I don't say anything
Because they'll follow me out and we'll both fall through
They'll hold my hand to save me and
I'll repay them with darkness and disaster
But even so I'm begging you
Please don't let me die here in Lancaster

13

Al got down the hill and collapsed fully clothed on his bed and slept. When he woke, it was midday. He was hungover and sore when he got up and looked out the window. The horse was still there and a hard wind blew down the canyon. There was no choice left but to make the thirty-mile walk to Morton's ranch to get help. So that's what he would do. He put more things in his backpack: the tequila, another can of soup, a pack of matches, and a lighter. He refilled his canteen. In a plastic storage tote he found new batteries for the portable radio and replaced them. A Mormon station out of Provo came in the strongest, and he set the radio outside under a sagebrush ten feet from the horse. He turned the volume up as loud as it could handle in hope that the sound might somehow scare a predator away. "I'm going to get you help. You just have to hang on a bit longer," he said to the horse, and left.

The elevation lowered and the aspen trees which lined the canyon creek disappeared and the canyon walls ended and the foothills began. In front of him were miles of snow-covered sagebrush that led to the desolate valley floor below.

He came to a lone pinyon pine fifty yards off the road and stopped.

He'd once blown a tire right where he was. He and Maxine had been at the claim for three days visiting Mel. They had decided to go into town and get a room for a night. They played bingo at the Elks Lodge, slots at the Tonopah Station, and stayed at the haunted Mizpah Hotel. In the morning they did Mel's laundry and grocery-shopped, and on the drive back, the right rear tire blew. It was midsummer and Al emptied the trunk and found the jack and lug wrench, pulled out the spare, and got to work.

"Jesus, it's hot today," Maxine said as she watched.

"I'm the one working," Al said. "Think how I feel."

"Well, you gotta be good for something," she said, and looked out over the valley. "I really like it here."

"Me, too."

"You know what I've always wanted to do?"

"What?"

"I've always wanted to walk in the middle of the desert naked. I knew a girl once who covered herself in mud at Pyramid Lake and walked around like that for hours. I've always wanted to do that."

"I think you should."

"We don't have any mud."

"Do it without mud."

"What if somebody comes?"

Al laughed. "Nobody will come."

"How do you know?"

"Because there's no one out here."

"You promise?"

"Yes."

"Then I'm gonna do it. But don't leave me, and don't laugh at me."

"I'd leave you but I only have three tires and I won't laugh because I love your body."

"At least somebody does." She looked around one more time and then took off her shorts and underwear, her T-shirt and bra. "How long you gonna be?"

"I'll honk when I'm getting ready."

"I'm gonna head up toward that tree."

"Okay."

"And you won't leave me?"

"No." Al laughed. "I won't leave you."

The sun appeared and was lost to clouds and appeared again and the wind howled and Al began walking. He hummed tunes and took short drinks off the tequila bottle. An old song came to him. A tune written in one day, played live just one night, and then discarded on a pile of other discarded songs. A country tune written for one gig, he supposed. "The Dice and Me." He was surprised that he remembered it, but he did and began to sing. A voice not good enough for anything but explaining a song. If he'd ever had the guts to leave Reno and had a better voice, maybe things would have turned out different. Maybe his songs would have found their way into the world easier. Maybe then he could have decided his own way of living instead of always jumping in on someone else's. As a side player he'd had to follow what the leader of the band wanted, what they thought was right. Touring for how long they wanted to tour. Touring where they wanted to tour. Practicing when they wanted to, not practicing when he wanted to, and always taking gigs only they wanted. But then there was nothing he could do about his voice.

THE DICE AND ME

I lost jobs when I was a kid
I'd get pissed off and that would be it
I spent my time drifting around
Nothing came through until I hit that Vegas town
I had a sleeping bag and an alleyway
All day long I'd roll the dice and work my game

The Dice and Me
The Dice and Me
You better watch out
For the Dice and Me

The lights of the city were no friends of mine
But the lights of the casino treated me more than kind
I ended up living in a hotel suite
With a cocktail waitress named Darlene
We'd be up all night and we'd sleep all day
The money rolled in and I made plans to stay

The Dice and Me
The Dice and Me
You better watch out
For the Dice and Me

But a gambler's life is holding a grenade
It's a tightrope act with a suicide weight
My Darlene she was on the grift
Stole my thirty grand and gave me the slip
And the dice ran cold because the dice could see
I was shaking from booze and my heart was ailing me

If I had any advice this is what it would be
Cut out your heart so the dice can't see

He'd written the song when he was twenty-four. The lyrics scribbled in a notebook while sitting in the bathtub. The
heart of the music, the style, came from the Buck Owens song
"I've Got a Tiger by the Tail." Two days after he finished it, he
played a pickup gig in Winnemucca at a Basque restaurant and
bar called the Winnemucca Hotel. The band, the Barbed Wire
Boys, were four guys in their forties with straight jobs. Part-
time musicians who did nothing but covers, but a week before
their Friday-night gig in Winnemucca and their Saturday night
in Elko their lead guitar player, who sang half the songs, broke
his collarbone in a motorcycle accident. Their drummer, who
had played for a time with Mona Maverick, gave Al a call to fill
in, and Al took the gig.

The majority of the songs he knew, and on the ones he
didn't, he held back. The band got through the first set, but
by the end of the second, they were running low on tunes the
remaining singer knew the lyrics to. By the third set, his voice
had begun to give out. They asked Al if he had any songs he
could sing. He told them he'd just written one called "The Dice
and Me" and told the guys the chords, gave the drummer the
tempo, and they tried it out.

The Winnemucca Hotel bar was a small rectangle room,
and the four-piece band was crammed in the corner on a two-
foot-high plywood stage. It was July and there was no air-
conditioning and the place was packed with nearly a hundred
people. But it was one of those nights that a band sometimes
stumbles upon—it doesn't matter if they are a good band or a

bad band but a night when they can do no wrong, a night when, for whatever reason, the audience loves them.

Al sang "The Dice and Me" and his thin voice was clear and loud through the PA. The band stumbled through the changes watching Al's fingers as he played, and by the end a strange thing happened. The place went crazy with applause. In front of the stage stood a small man in khaki shorts and a red polyester collared shirt. "Goddamn!" he yelled over the din of the bar. He was bald and had no eyebrows and no hair on his arms or face. His teeth were small and yellow, he had a nose that had been broken, freckled skin, and glassed-over eyes. He waved Al over. "Come here, bud!"

Al stepped between the monitors and leaned down.

"I'll give you a hundred bucks if you play that one again."

Al laughed and shook his head.

"I'm serious." The bald man took a hundred-dollar bill from a roll of money and waved it around. The guys in the band nodded and Al got back on the mic.

"This man wants to hear that last song again. It's a new one for us, would you mind if we tried it one more time?"

The place cheered and Al counted it off. The band played it better that time and the bald man stayed in front and tried to sing along. He had a bottle of beer in his hand and another in his back pocket. When they finished, the place again went crazy and the bald man jumped onstage. He pulled out his roll of money and this time took two hundred-dollar bills from it. "You gotta play that song one more time," he yelled.

"Don't give us any more money," Al told him. "You'll be in a mess of shit tomorrow when you realize what you've done."

"I ain't drunk, and I got money," he said, and put the bills in

Al's suit coat pocket. "Money talks and bullshit walks. Play it one more time."

Al shook his head.

The man turned to the bar of people and said into Al's mic, "That last song, that song is my song. I swear to God it was written for me. But these boys won't play it again and I need to hear it. Please, just one more time." After that he began yelling into the mic, "One more time, one more time, one more time!" Soon the entire room of people in that dilapidated bar screamed, "One more time!"

The bald man jumped off the stage and the band played it again. When they finished it that time, the bald man went to the bar and came back with a bottle of Jameson and four beers and set them on the stage while the band ran through Hank Cochran's "Life of a Rodeo Cowboy."

The set ended, the bartender started the jukebox, and Al went outside. The summer night was breezy and warm and he could see Main Street and the colored lights of Winners Casino and the semitrucks and cars passing through town. He sat on the sidewalk, and the sounds of music and people talking and laughing drifted from inside. He nursed a beer and cooled down and the bald man came outside, lit a cigarette, and walked over to him. "You don't know how much that song meant to me," the man said. "Did you write it?"

"Yeah," Al said.

"You got it recorded?"

"No."

"You going to?"

"I don't know."

"Well, I'm a professional gambler. I make my living betting

sports but I live for the dice. I live for the table. That song really hit me."

"Thanks," Al said. "And everyone in the band thanks you . . . You from around here?"

"I'm from everywhere and nowhere," the man said, and smiled. "I'm what you'd call a mover. I'm always moving, always on the road. But that's the way I like it." He took the roll of money from his pocket, counted out ten hundred-dollar bills, and dropped them on the pavement in front of Al. "You'll probably be playing these dumps your entire life. That's hard work, and you wrote a hell of a song. Hopefully these greenbacks help you out."

Al looked at the bills. "I can't take that."

"You'll take it. Money ain't nothing to me. Thanks again for the tune," he said, and walked away.

The next morning Al woke up at the Scott Shady Court Motel. It was dawn and he had his own room. He lay in bed playing the Telecaster and working on a song called "Mr. Luck and Ms. Doom." At eight he walked to the Griddle restaurant for breakfast. He was dressed in a black suit with a crisp new gray-and-black-pin-striped western shirt underneath, shiny black boots, and his hair slicked back with pomade. He wasn't hungover, his nerves were good, and he had over a thousand dollars in his pocket.

In a booth that looked out over Main Street he ate breakfast. The waitress, a young blonde, flirted with him and gave him a free orange juice. The sun hadn't yet risen over the town and the morning was still cool when he left. The band was driving to Elko at noon and he hoped he could see an afternoon matinee before the gig. He passed the street of his motel and kept walking. Across the road was Winners Casino and it was there he saw the bald-headed man with no eyebrows in a green polyester shirt and black shorts walking with a young boy dressed exactly the same. They were holding hands and Al guessed they were heading to the Griddle for breakfast. He waved from across the four-lane road but semitrucks and cars got in the way and the man and boy didn't see him and just kept walking.

14

It was ten miles to get to the main gravel road. From there Morton's ranch was twenty miles north at the far edge of the long valley. In every direction as far as he could see was snow-covered sagebrush. The only sounds were the wind and his boots breaking through snow. He had walked for five hours when his legs began to shake and he had to stop. In the middle of the road he sat and drank off the tequila bottle and ate bites of snow.

He tried not to think of the past but he could no longer control his thoughts. His mind went where it wanted, when it wanted, no matter how hard he tried to stop it. He remembered after Lancaster being in Mel's truck on that same road. How Mel had him work the mine to get his strength back. Mel cooking for him, Mel trying in his own way to talk to Al and help him. It took over a month before Al felt strong enough to go back to Reno, and the day he left they went to Nevada State Bank in Tonopah and Mel transferred ten thousand dollars into Al's account.

"It aged you this time. So take care of yourself," Mel said.

"I'll try . . . I owe you, Mel."

"No, you don't owe me. Just remember, underneath the bottle's beauty, it's a mean motherfucker."

Al laughed and for the first time in his life he hugged his great-uncle before he got on the bus and left.

In Reno he called the number of the man in Lancaster who

owned his guitar. He begged for the Telecaster back. "I was in rough shape that day," he said. "I'm embarrassed. I really am but . . . Shit, I've had that guitar since I was fourteen. I've been gigging with it for forty-three years. Would you sell it back to me?"

"I don't know," the man said.

"Please," Al said. "I'll pay you a grand for it."

"It's worth a lot more than that."

"Yeah," Al said. "I guess it is . . . I'll pay you two grand."

"Make it three."

The next morning Al drove seven hours to Lancaster. The man lived in a nondescript 1990s subdivision. He was waiting for Al in a lawn chair outside his open garage, the guitar case next to him. Al couldn't remember the man at all. Not one thing about him was familiar. Without talking, Al took three thousand dollars from his pants pocket and handed it to him. The man counted it and gave Al the case. Al opened it to see Herb Marks's Telecaster inside. He touched it, closed the case, and left. He was so happy and relieved that at times tears welled in his eyes. He drove straight back to Reno and didn't stop, not even for a break, until he'd gotten out of California.

The afternoon's warmth began to fade and the sky behind him, toward the mountains and the claim, grew dark with storm clouds. He thought again of the horse. Soon it would be engulfed in it, alone and blind in a snowstorm. Al forced himself up. His feet were numb, his knees hurt, and in front of him was nothing but miles of desolate valley. It all seemed so hopeless, but he kept on and sang tunes as he went: Merle Haggard's "Going Where the Lonely Go" and Sammi Smith's "Jimmy's in Georgia" and the Los Lobos version of "I Got Loaded." The songs drifted in and out and he sang one he'd written called "The Big Escape," an up-tempo cowpunk tune he'd written for his band The Sanchez Brothers. It was a tune that had never made a record but one he had always liked. A song about the night Vern had taken Al to Kilroys diner in the Nevada Club and told him of his plan for them to move to Kansas City.

It was fall and a Saturday, Al was twelve years old, and they sat in the last two available seats at a long counter. On a napkin, Vern had Al write what he was going to take with him. "Don't take too much stuff," his uncle said, and took a long drink off a beer. "Just enough so you got your things. Think one suitcase. And we'll need a car . . ."

He also told Al to prewrite a letter to his mother explaining that they were leaving and for her not to worry. "Have it ready," Vern said, "because we could be heading out any day. Any day . . . Pretty soon you won't have to live with Ms. Stick Up Her Ass anymore and we'll be rolling down the road free and easy."

Their lunch came and Vern told Al how Kansas City was a good railroad town. He left his lunch untouched, ordered another beer, and said he'd get back on a union rail crew. He'd buy them a house, and when Al turned sixteen, he'd get Al on the same crew and they'd work together and would be set for the rest of their lives.

Al went home and wrote the letter to his mother and for weeks after he dreamed of nothing but he and Vern running away. He was so excited that he stayed up late each night waiting and began falling asleep in class. He gave up on his schoolwork. But when he saw Vern next, his uncle didn't bring up Kansas City or the house they were going to buy. It was on

Virginia Street, outside of Harolds Club, and Al ran up to him and broke down crying on the sidewalk, begging Vern to tell him when they were leaving.

"Leaving for where?"

"Kansas City!" Al said with tears streaming down his face.

"Why the hell do you want to go to Kansas City?"

"That's where you said we were going."

"I said?" Vern laughed.

"You promised."

"Well . . ." He rubbed his face with his hands. "Shit, Al, I don't remember saying that. I'm sorry. But I tell you, I wouldn't mind living in Kansas City. I hear they got cheap houses and good barbecue and they have a lot of trains there. We could probably get on a crew pretty easy."

15

After his divorce from Maxine was finalized, Al's nerves once again gave out. He played no gigs and thought his life as a musician was over. At night he quit going to clubs and bars, and he quit answering his phone. He went through his savings and got a job as a breakfast cook at a place called Little Sam's. From six a.m. to two p.m. he worked five days a week. Outside of that he began living half drunk. Drunk enough so his nerves would let him go to a store and do the things he had to do to get by, but not so drunk that he wouldn't be able to get up and go to work in the morning.

His life went like that for over a year, until one afternoon, while he was sitting at the Little Sam's bar having an after-shift drink, two men came in. Both were young and over six feet three inches tall, rail-thin, and handsome. They looked like Mexican movie stars from the 1950s. Each had thick greased-back black hair and wore cowboy boots. Their jeans were black and narrowed at the calf. One wore a black T-shirt, and on it was printed a large *X* on fire. Above and to the left of the *X* it said *Los Angeles*. The other wore a black short-sleeve western pearl-snap-button shirt and had a tattoo of a horseshoe on his forearm.

The one in the T-shirt said, "You're Al Ward, right?"

Al nodded.

The man in the western shirt said, "We really like the tunes of yours we've found. 'Roll Reno Roll'; 'Layover in Tokyo';

'High Time We Quit This Low Living'; 'Tapped Out in Tulsa'; 'Walking by the House Where I Used to Live'; 'When the Clock Strikes Three and I'm Not Home'; and 'Hard Living, Hard Drinking, Hard Times.'"

Al laughed. "How the hell do you guys know those songs?"

The one in the T-shirt said, "Our dad tried to find all the records you were a part of. He really liked you."

"Are you still writing?" the one in the western shirt asked.

"Not really," Al said. "I've given it up."

"Why would you do that?"

Al shrugged.

"Can we buy you a drink?"

Al nodded and they moved to a table in the back of the bar.

"We're The Sanchez Brothers. I mean that's the name of the band. I'm Lou," the one in the T-shirt said. "And this is my brother, Jaime. I play guitar and he plays bass. We have a bad-ass drummer but we're looking for another guitar player and for someone to help us write songs. Writing songs is what we're worst at. We sing like the Everly Brothers, no shit, we're that good. But the songs we have suck."

"They don't all suck," Jaime said.

"He's wrong. They do."

"I agree, most of them suck, but they don't all suck. What about 'A Horse Named Hair Trigger'?"

Lou laughed. "That's an instrumental of ours. We wrote it about our dad's old horse, Hair Trigger. Our pop broke both arms on him when he was our age."

"He was younger than that."

"He was close enough to our age."

"Not really," Jaime said.

Lou gave his brother a look. "Anyway, it's our best song, but it's an instrumental. And the thing is, we're singers. We like punk rock, but we grew up on country and all kinds of other shit. Our dad was obsessed with music. He was a great guitar player and he always talked about you. He said you were the only guy in town who cared about writing tunes, the only one around here who was the 'real deal.' That was the term he used. He used to follow your career and that's how we know about you."

"What's his name?"

"Paul Sanchez," Lou said. "Maybe you met him."

"I don't remember him, but if I saw him, I bet I'd recognize him."

"He's dead now," Jaime said.

"I'm sorry to hear that."

The brothers nodded.

"Anyway," Jaime said, "we live with our mom off Holcomb and Wheeler. There's two houses on the lot and we stay in the back one and practice in the basement."

"Will you come over and hear us play and maybe join us?" Lou asked.

Al shook his head. "I'm too old for you guys."

"How old are you?" Jaime asked.

"I just turned forty."

The brothers looked at each other and laughed.

"Shit," Lou said. "We didn't know you were that old."

"Fuck, that is old," Jaime said.

"But you still look cool," Lou said. He glanced at his brother and his brother nodded. "We don't care if you're an old man. And just so you know, we want to be a big-time band."

Jaime shook his head.

"It's true, ain't it?"

"Yeah, it's true. It just sounds lame when you say it."

"All I know is we want to be a national touring act that has records. Not a nothing local band, you know?"

"And we don't want to play no casino bullshit, either," added Jaime.

"Those gigs have dried up, anyway," Al said. "Casinos don't care about live music anymore. They were bad gigs, but the money was good."

"We're too wild for that shit," Jaime said.

"We're too loud and too fast," Lou added, and smiled. "We want to be the Mexican Everly Brothers on speed."

"We want to be Simon and Garfunkel but punk rock and pissed off. Fast and badass but we sing like saints," Jaime said.

"He's right we do."

"How old are you guys?"

"I'm twenty-two and Jaime's twenty."

"Well, I'd like to hear what you guys got going on, because me, I got nothing."

Three days later Al sat in a folding chair in the brothers' basement. The walls of the room were covered in carpet remnants to deaden the sound. Taped to the ceiling were flyers for bands Al had never heard of playing clubs he didn't know existed. There were beer and Coke cans on the floor and an old black dog named Red who lay curled in a ball, unbothered, while the band bashed away.

The drummer was a twenty-three-year-old metalhead named Wayne Jenson, nicknamed "Bic" because he chain-smoked hand-rolled cigarettes and always carried Bic lighters. He lived with his mother in Sparks, delivered pizzas using her car, and practiced daily to Iron Maiden, Saxon, Judas Priest, and Rush records in her garage.

The brothers' harmonies were flawless, they were good musicians, but they were right, they didn't have songs. When the rehearsal ended, they took a cooler of beer from the basement to the backyard, where Mrs. Sanchez, a woman only a few years older than Al, was barbecuing chicken. She was a high school English teacher and white and lanky with brown hair held in a haphazard bun. She wore flip-flops and a green muumuu. Ornette Coleman played on a stereo from the main house and they all ate together at a picnic table under a tin-roofed awning.

"We've been excited to have you here," Mrs. Sanchez said. "My husband and I knew about you. We used to watch you with Lynda and Lacy and before that Rex Winchester. And also with the big guy."

"Ronnie Willis?"

"That's him. I really like the way he sings. It's like one song he's Waylon Jennings and the next he's Otis Redding."

"Yeah, he can do anything," Al said.

"I don't see him around anymore."

"No, you wouldn't. He moved back to Carson City a while ago and lives in his mom's garage. He battles depression and quits music every so often and this is one of those times. He must have broken up the band ten times when I played with him. But I love the way he sings."

"I bet you're a good singer," she said, and smiled.

"I'm not tone-deaf, but I'm not much better than that."

"Bob Dylan is her favorite singer," Jaime said. "So if you can't sing, she'd probably love your voice."

"I like good singers, but they don't all have to be Aretha Franklin," Mrs. Sanchez said. "I just know I'd like Al's voice because his songs are sad and I like sad songs and sad singers the best."

Al laughed. "You're one of the few."

"I'm serious." She again smiled and she didn't take her eyes off him. "I could tell by the first song I heard of yours that I'd like you."

"Really?" he said.

"I'm the one that bought all your singles. You write with a broken heart and I understand broken hearts."

"Thank you," he said.

"That's her way of flirting, Al," Jaime said, and everyone laughed.

"I'm an English teacher," she said. "What do you expect?"

"Our mom and dad followed all the good musicians in town and he liked you the best, too," Lou said.

"And he was a great guitar player," Jaime said. "He could have been famous. He could have hung with Chet Atkins but he loved Ma too much."

"It wasn't me," Mrs. Sanchez said. "He was just a homebody. He liked being home at night with you guys and he liked stability."

"And there's not much stability in being in a band," Al said.

"I wouldn't imagine there is," she said.

"But your sons are really good."

"You think so?"

"Yeah."

"We got a brand-new van, too," Lou said.

"It's parked in the alley out back," Jaime said.

"When my husband died, he left us some money through an insurance policy and I saved it. I didn't want them touring in the van they had."

"I was scared just going to the store in the last one," Bic said.

"We called it Stalker Van," Jaime added. "Because it looked like the kind a stalker would live in."

"And it had an exhaust leak, so you had to drive with the windows down even in the winter," Lou said, and they laughed at that and ate and drank and talked. They listened to records by the Everly Brothers, the Blasters, Merle Haggard, Rank and File, Rush, Gram Parsons, X, Charlie Parker, Los Lobos, Black Sabbath, and Jimmy Bryant & Speedy West. Afterward the brothers walked Al to the duplex and again asked him to join their band, and Al was so swept up in them and the night that he told them he'd give it a try.

The rehearsals were twice a week and on breaks they would sit in the backyard and drink beer and Al would listen to their conversations. He picked out stories they would tell, phrases they'd use, and began writing songs around those. Because of the long practices and the early shifts at Little Sam's, Al began sleeping through the night and his nerves eased. He kept his drinking in check and once again carried a notebook and wrote down lyrics and song ideas. He wrote at work and on his walk home, in the bathtub, and in front of the TV at night.

They practiced and played no gigs and because of that the songs came. "Juanita, I Want You Bad"; "The Needle Ain't No Friend"; "Stabbing at the Nevada Club"; "Marianne's in the Mental Ward"; "Living on the Streets of San Francisco"; "The Disappearance of Paco Ramírez"; "Skinheads on Sutro"; "Can't You See I'm Dying, Maxine"; "Swastika on My Mom's Front Door"; "The All Night Every Night Beaner Goodtime Rag"; "The Mexican Girl"; "Waiting for You to Get Off the Bus"; "Susie, Wanda, Roxy & Lee"; "The Police Pullover on Christmas Eve"; "I Won't Let Anything Happen to You"; "The Cowpunk Breakdown."

Al and Bic began practicing on their own to tinker on song arrangements. Bic told Al that the fewer decisions the brothers had to make, the fewer arguments between them there would be. "You're just starting to see it now because they've been on their best behavior. They want you in the band so bad they're trying not to fight around you. They did the same thing to me. They saw me playing with this metal band called Saw Cutter. The band really sucked and the brothers were so cool and could sing so good I started playing with them and quit Saw Cutter. I grew up on the Everly Brothers, they're my mom's favorite, so I was an easy mark. I joined and then, well . . . Those mother-fuckers are always fighting. They're like best buddies and all is good and then the next second they'll be beating the shit out of each other. I'm not joking. At the drop of a hat, bam! Especially when they're on speed."

"Speed?" asked Al.

"Shit, man, why do you think they always want me to play so fast? When you're not around, every other word is *cocaine* or *crystal*. But they don't want you to think they're drug addicts. So whatever you do, don't tell them I told you or they'll start picking on me."

"I won't. I just thought it was so fast because it's that style of music," Al said. "Punk rock."

"Maybe, but not really. Before you joined, there'd be times when I'd be back there and we'd be halfway through a song and they'd just start yelling at me to go faster. So I'd be going and going and then suddenly they'd be at each other's throats trying to kill each other. Mid-song sometimes."

Al rubbed his face with his hands.

"I'm telling you all this because it's gonna blow up any time now. I can feel it and you should be ready for it. I mean those guys can only act normal for so long."

"I didn't know."

"That's because they don't want you to know. They're scared you'll quit. But as soon as you leave practice, it starts. I'm telling you, man, the second you're heading home, bam!" Bic lit a cigarette and smiled. "They don't want you to know because they think you're the shit. And you are. These songs are awesome. How do you write so many?"

"I don't know," Al said. "I got nothing else to do and I work at it a lot. Since I was a kid I've been like that."

"You just started writing them?"

Al nodded. "I'd had a guitar a couple months and one night I wrote a song that was a rip-off of an old Ferlin Husky tune called 'Draggin' the River.' I wrote the lyrics for 'Bonnie Let's Run Away' about this girl in my geometry class. I spent weeks on that tune but those were the only lyrics I could come up with." He stopped and let out a small laugh. "But it was like working on a puzzle, and the whole time I'm trying to figure it out, the world stops, I'm with Bonnie, and I don't think about anything else. I was just in there chasing this thing, which is a good song. It's addicting."

"Unless you write a shitty one."

Al laughed again. "Sadly, most of mine are. But once in a while you get lucky. There's a guy, I can't remember who, but he said that when you write a good tune and you know it's good, and you haven't played it for anyone, it's like holding hope in your pocket. And the hope has a heart that's beating and it rushes through you and all around you. For a moment you're proud of yourself because you have this little bit of gold that no one's heard and you're the only guy in the world that knows it or feels it or knows how good the tune is. That's the best feeling."

"How many times you felt that?"

"A few, maybe. The problem is it goes away as soon as you start playing it to people and get tired of it. After that you're off chasing another, hoping it'll happen again. I guess it's like anything . . . Are they going to start yelling at me?"

"Probably, but it won't be too bad. I mean they even like the ballads you bring in, especially 'Juanita, I Want You Bad.' But don't bring in too many because then they really will start yelling at you."

"Shit," Al said. "I get tired of playing fast."

"You get tired of playing fast? Man, I gotta play that train-beat shit all the time, and when I finally get off that trip, they make me play whatever else at breakneck speed. Before you started, if I wasn't going fast enough they'd start yelling at me. Lou's line was 'Faster, motherfucker, faster!' But I'm not complaining, and the brothers are really cool when they're cool. Especially when it's just one of them you're talking to. And we're the best band in town for sure. Especially with your songs. And shit, who else in town am I gonna play with? It's either this or I play in some shit-ass metal band or go back to my garage and play along to records."

The band rehearsed for eight months and then, before playing even a single gig, they drove to Los Angeles and recorded and mixed sixteen songs in eight days at a studio the brothers had arranged and paid for with their father's insurance money. By the end of the session, they had also somehow secured a booking agent and a record deal with a small independent Los Angeles label. They came home and everyone arranged five weeks off work to go on the road to promote their first record. The Sanchez Brothers, *Reno*.

"Jesus, I'm too old to do these dates the way you want to," Al said when he saw the itinerary of thirty-five shows in thirty-six days. "I can't couch-surf and drink all night in some guy's house and then get up and sit in a van all day, load in, and play a gig. I need a motel room. A Motel 6 or worse, just drop me off and pick me up. You can all take showers there in the morning. But I can't couch-surf. My nerves will give out and I can't afford that. But I got money. I'll pay for the room."

The brothers agreed and the band went on the road. Because it was their van, Jaime and Lou insisted on driving and sitting in front. The brothers bickered over the radio, over which gas station to stop at, which restaurant to eat at, where they should park, and what time they should leave in the morning. They first fought backstage at a club in Wichita and then in the parking lot of an IHOP in Oklahoma City. After the second fight Bic told the brothers to designate Al the band leader so they wouldn't have to make so many decisions. They agreed and Al became the road manager. He decided where they would eat, he advanced shows, he separated the brothers from selling merchandise together, he began settling money with the clubs and holding the band's bank.

Lou and Jaime's father was an electrician who died of a heart attack when they were in middle school. Bic's father was an unemployed manic-depressive who lived at the Donner Inn Motel in Reno. So Al became a sort of father figure to the three. Separately they each went to him when they had a problem, band-related or not, and Al tried his best to help. He tried to be a good influence. He drank only after the gigs, never got too loaded, and never lost his temper. He kept his darkness to himself and tried to be a good cheerleader. What he realized as he sat in the van day after day was that it was the first band he had ever been in that made no money, but it was the first band where he believed in the music. He believed in The Sanchez Brothers.

When Lou and Jaime got in the van each morning haggard and hungover from the night before, he said things like, "Look, I like boozing, too, and the sad thing is I probably been drunk longer than you guys been alive, but let's do our job first and our serious drinking at home. We're sitting in this van all day for one reason and that is to promote the record and show everyone that a band from Reno, Nevada, can be the shit. Remember, we have to deliver every single night at every single gig." The brothers and even Bic would laugh when Al said such things. They began calling him the Old Man. But he knew they liked hearing the things he said, and he knew they helped. Besides the years he was married to Maxine, it was one of the few times in his life when he was proud of himself. Proud of what he was doing and how he was acting. He was writing good songs, he was trying as hard as he could, he cared about his bandmates, and never once for their entire run as a band did he knowingly let them down.

But the brothers were wild. They had never been away from home, and each night on that first tour, even if they weren't getting along or the gig was not well attended, they got drunk and did drugs together if they could find them. Bic and Al began driving the day shifts so the brothers could sleep. By the end of the second week Bic had to force the brothers up at whatever house they were staying in and they would yell and throw things at him and always they were late in picking Al up at the motel.

At a diner in Opelousas, Louisiana, Bic and Al sat across from each other eating lunch while the brothers slept in the van.

"What the hell do they do every night?"

"You don't want to know."

"I don't," Al said. "But I guess I sorta need to know. I ain't judging, but they look worse every day. So what do you guys do?"

"Don't include me," Bic said. "Usually I just drink beer and find some part of the house we're staying in that's quiet and then I get in my sleeping bag and read."

"What do you read?"

"Right now I'm reading the *Master and Commander* series. You ever read it?"

"No."

"It's about a sea captain named Aubrey, it's really good. Other than that, I just try to sleep."

"What about Lou and Jaime?"

"Chicks love them and they love chicks. Why do you think they dress so good? They stay up all night doing blow or any kind of speed they can get and hook up with women if they can. They drink a fuck ton, too. You can drink twice as much on that shit, and man, they really do."

Al set down his fork and put his elbows on the table. "Do you think they'll make it through the tour?"

Bic laughed. "We have twelve days left. I have no idea. I mean you know them as good as I do now."

Al sat back and sighed.

With a mouthful of food Bic said, "I can't believe people really like us."

"Me, neither."

"I think it's the only reason the brothers haven't killed each other for real."

"How you holding up?"

"Honestly, Al, I wouldn't mind staying in the motel room once in a while. I get tired of the weirdos we stay with. Last night I was in a closet because it was the only quiet place, but part of me kept thinking they'd lock me in there. It was that kind of homestay, a house with four punk rock guys and a party going on. I think they were junkies, too, and the toilet was fucking gross. It was just . . . And the shower was so moldy I wore my shoes in there, that's why they're wet. But man, I sweat so much playing that I don't sleep good unless I take a shower. So I had to. And that house, in the main room, was a huge aquarium and inside it was a dead iguana floating in the water and dead fish on the bottom. Iguanas don't live in water. It was seriously sketchy, man. You think maybe I could stay on the motel room floor sometimes? I wouldn't bother you, it's just so I can sleep. Maybe we could talk those guys into trusting us with the van and we could drop them off."

"That's a good idea," Al said. "We'll get a room with two beds. I'm sorry, I didn't know. I thought you liked partying and staying out with the guys."

"Maybe once in a while, but mostly I just like being someplace where I can read and I won't get killed or get lice and where there's a lock on the bathroom door. The other night we were staying in this warehouse and I was on the can and these two girls walked in. One of them I'd been trying to talk to. You should have seen the look on her face. It was so embarrassing, man, and the chick was really cute."

There were times in the van when everyone was awake and they discussed what was working and what wasn't with the set, what mistakes were being made, and which songs to cut and which to add. Even hungover and undone the brothers wanted to be better, for the set to be better, because the band was working and they knew it. They could win over crowds who didn't know them, and the reviews of the record began coming in with four and five stars. Magazines and punk rock fanzines were starting to cover them, and after only two weeks of gigs they had to have the label ship them more LPs and cassettes. They also ran through their T-shirts, and the brothers, who had brought a silk-screen kit with them, made new ones on the road.

They went as far east as Atlanta before working their way back west. They played New Orleans, Houston, Austin, Dallas, El Paso, Albuquerque, Tucson, Phoenix, and Las Vegas. When the tour ended, Al handed them each three hundred dollars. He'd lost seven pounds and went back to work at Little Sam's run-down and exhausted.

Two months later they went out again. Twenty-six shows in twenty-seven days. This time Al had to quit his job and began dipping into his savings to make it work. He also made rules. There would be no drinking or drugs until a half hour before the show. They had to have one sit-down meal a day and there would be no overnight drives. Bic was designated the after-the-gig driver and was to take the van to the motel where he and Al would share a room. Al told the brothers they could do what they wanted but he recommended they take at least a couple nights off a week and on those nights they'd get an extra room.

The brothers fought first in a Safeway parking lot in Denver. Al and Bic had to break it up. They didn't hurt their hands or mouths to the point where they couldn't play or sing but Jaime broke Lou's nose and Lou sang the next week with two black eyes and a swollen face. The fight scared even the brothers and for a time they quit arguing and the gigs went on. The clubs were small but they played a nearly sold-out show their first time in Chicago and again in Madison and Milwaukee.

At the end of that tour Al got out of the van with two hundred dollars and a drinking habit of a pint of tequila a day. He'd lost the seven pounds he'd gained back, had just turned forty-one, and was laid out flat in bed sick for five days. He sold his 1974 Les Paul to pay his bills and began subbing at Little Sam's.

The band played a local show at a bar called the Blue Max, and Al met Colleen Langston, a thirty-one-year-old part-time prostitute. Colleen was short and curvy with dyed black hair and was covered in tattoos at a time when most women didn't have even one. She was obsessed with punk rock and bebop jazz, had an addiction to painkillers and Valium, and was the sort of alcoholic who put vodka in her coffee when she woke. Her childhood, she told Al, was spent in Los Angeles with her grandmother. She moved out when she was thirteen and had done time in prison for drug possession and prostitution. She told Al she no longer lived that life, but she would vanish for days and never explain where she went. Al had no idea what she did or how she had money, and after a time he quit asking.

They'd been together six months when she broke down crying in bed, telling Al she loved him. "I been with a lot of guys, Al, but you're the only one I feel like is my friend. You seem so heartbroken all the time. I love drinking with you and listening to music with you. I love when you cook for me and play guitar. I just love you to pieces. I really do."

Al told Colleen he loved her back and he supposed in a way he did. She could be funny and sweet and sometimes kind. She was tough and streetwise and had a doomed-prisoner outlook in everything she saw and he felt comfort in that. Colleen was also the first woman Al had been with since Maxine. With her, he realized just how lonely and isolated he had become since his divorce. But Colleen worried him. She had never held a straight job and seemed to be working an angle in every situation they were in. At times it felt like he didn't know her at all. But she didn't ask for much, she liked the way he lived his life, and he got used to her disappearing and then showing up run-down and ragged in the middle of the night.

The band went out again, twenty-eight dates in thirty days, and then did a short two-week run of the West Coast before taking an extended break of eight months. Off the road they rehearsed two nights a week and worked on the new songs that Al would bring in. The brothers scheduled time at the same studio in Los Angeles, and as a safeguard Mrs. Sanchez rode in the van and stayed with her sons while they cut thirteen songs. "Uno, Dos, Tres—I'm Gonna Bust Your Face"; "When You Gonna Sleep, Colleen?"; "I Can't Trust No One"; "Henrietta, I'll Love You Forever"; "Slow Down, Salvador Sánchez, Slow Down"; "Watch Out, Perlita—He's Got a Knife"; "The Ballad of the Trujillo Brothers"; "The Beating of a Mexican Kid on 4th Street"; "The Dishwasher's Lament"; "Living in My Car"; "Bonnie Blacked Out Again"; "Ándale, Motherfucker, Ándale"; "Walking You Home Through the Bad Part of Town."

When the recording finished, they drove back to Reno, and again Al subbed at Little Sam's, worked on songs, and spent his free time with Colleen. But he began noticing things missing from his apartment. Records he didn't like, an extra set of speakers he didn't use, an old TV he kept in a closet. Each time he confronted her, Colleen would cop to it and begin crying.

"You don't have to put on an act," Al told her after she stole one of his spare guitars, a black 1977 Telecaster. "You know and I know what you're doing. So don't cry and make a big deal out of it. I'm dumb but not dumb like that. Look, I can give you money when I got it, at least as much as you get hawking a bunch of shit that's not worth anything. The guitar is the first thing that hurt a little. I like being with you and I like having you here. You make my life better and I hope I make your life better. We're both fucked up, but even so there's always gotta be a line you can't cross and you're starting to cross it. If we really are friends, you can't steal my shit or we'll have to quit. It's just no way to live."

The second record, *4th Street Blackout,* was released. The label was small but put more money behind it and the reviews again came out with four and five stars. The band lined up a series of tours to support it. Three weeks on two weeks off, five weeks on four weeks off, four weeks on four weeks off, and then three weeks on followed by a seven-month break to work on the third record. The band left in the same van and drove to the East Coast. They played half the shows on their own and the other half opening for another band. But no matter the night or the gig, the brothers never slowed. It was like a switch was turned on the second they got in the van and couldn't be turned off until they were back home. Al began taking each of them aside separately, begging them to ease up. Twice he came to tears. He had Bic talk to them, he had their mother talk to them.

On the outskirts of Cleveland, Ohio, Al was driving. Bic was in the passenger seat and the brothers sat on their own bench seats in the back of the van. They were arguing about a woman named Deidra Ryan who worked at a bar in Reno called Area 51. "It's just because she doesn't want to fuck you and she wants to fuck me," Jaime said from the backseat.

"I don't give a shit about her," Lou said from the front bench seat.

"You do give a shit. I can tell."

"I don't."

"I bet you'll call her tonight."

"Listen, motherfucker, I'm telling you to shut the fuck up."

"Why are you always in such a shit-ass mood when you wake up?"

"You're worse than me, you whine like a baby."

"That ain't fucking true and you know it. I can take it. I might be the little brother but I can take any hangover and still sing spot-on. You ain't got the balls I got, and that's why, brother, Deidra would rather fuck me than you."

"You ain't fucked her and you know it."

Bic, who had been reading a book, set it on his lap and turned around. "I know Deidra. She's married and her husband was in the marines. He's seriously tough. I'd bet a million dollars she wouldn't fuck either of you."

"But that's where you're wrong," Jaime said, and laughed. "She's fucked me three times. Twice when her husband was out of town and once in the storeroom of Area 51 when he was sitting at the bar. She's got a birthmark above her coochie that looks like a little bird, and believe me, I've stared at that motherfucker for a long time."

Bic turned back around and the van fell silent. Lou lay down on the bench seat and put his coat over his face. Minutes went by, the moment seemed to have passed, and then Lou erupted. He dove over the back of the seat and began hitting Jaime in the face. The overweighted van began to rock back and forth. Al eased them to the shoulder of the I-90 freeway as cars and semitrucks rushed past. It was nearly a half hour until they settled down enough for Al to continue driving. The brothers didn't speak to each other until that night's gig, and when they did, it was like nothing had happened.

The third tour for the second record was even better attended. The clubs were still small but were nearly always full. San Francisco, Portland, Seattle, Minneapolis, Madison, Milwaukee, Chicago, Ann Arbor, Detroit, Cleveland, Pittsburgh, Boston, and New York City. The brothers lost weight, their voices went out, and finally they quit being careful at all around Al.

"I can't believe the shit you guys say to each other," Al would tell them. "Don't you know how fucked up it is? And what's the point of it? You guys are brothers and you love each other. That's just a fact, so you gotta stop it before you really fuck each other up. I'm serious. I mean your dad would be so proud of you guys if he could see us playing, but I bet it would break his heart if he saw the way you guys treat each other. And your mom, Jesus, you have a mom who bought you a van and calls everyone she knows telling them to come out and see us, who sends you guys care packages on the road. If she knew, really knew, how you guys were out here, it would break her heart in a thousand pieces. I know it breaks mine . . . I mean, shit, I love you guys, I love you like you're my family. You guys saved me. You saved my life after my divorce, and you let me write real songs. And people like us. You don't know how rare and lucky that is, how rare it is that we all found each other. Goddamn, I just don't understand why you fuck with each other so hard. Just hour after hour after hour. Can you explain it to me? Please, explain it."

Neither of them could, and after a fistfight in the back of a Lawrence, Kansas, club, Lou and Jaime wouldn't speak to each other. Bic was used as a mediator and told Al he was thinking of going to college and getting out of music altogether. Al drank more and Bic began driving the morning shift. He listened to books on tape with a Walkman while Al slept off his hangover in the passenger seat and the brothers lay like the dead in the back.

In a Days Inn breakfast room on the outskirts of Salt Lake City, Al sat down across from Bic, who was eating a mixture of Raisin Bran, Froot Loops, and half-and-half. He was leaned over, his elbows on the table, his head down, as he shoveled the cereal into his mouth.

"Everything all right?" Al asked.

Bic shrugged.

"Who was calling you at six in the morning?"

Bic quit eating. "My dad. My mom knew we were staying here and must have told him. Sorry if it woke you."

"It's all right. Everything okay?"

Bic shook his head.

"What?"

"I don't want to bother you, man."

"You're not bothering me. I'm asking."

Bic wore a white T-shirt that read *Rank and File—Sundown* in red ink. His eyes were bloodshot. He had a cold and was pale under the fluorescent lights. He looked around the room and whispered, "It was my dad's birthday yesterday and he's all mad because no one made a big deal out of it. He'd been up all night stewing and being crazy and making calls to people. It was four a.m. in Reno when he called here. And shit, I called him two days ago and wished him happy birthday and I sent him a card when we were in St. Louis because I knew we were driving all day yesterday. But he didn't mention that. He just started yelling that I didn't care about him. And then I got pissed."

"What did you do?"

"I asked him when my birthday was."

"And he didn't know?"

"Nah, he didn't know." Bic got up and went to the buffet counter and made another bowl and sat back down. "What's your dad like?"

"I don't know him," Al said.

"You don't know him at all?"

"I don't even know who he is," Al said, and smiled. "I guess for a while my mom was a party gal. At least that's what my uncles told me. Drank a lot and ran around and . . . I guess she left town with some guy when she was seventeen and came home alone and pregnant when she was twenty-one."

"And she never told you who he was?"

Al took a sip of coffee and shook his head. "When I was a kid I used to ask but she'd get really pissed off so I quit asking. When she was dying, I asked again. But even then she wouldn't tell me. Now she's dead and I don't know . . . My uncle Mel told me right before she took off that he saw her walking down Virginia Street by Harolds Club arm in arm with an older man. The guy was tall like me and thin with black hair and blue eyes. So maybe it was him."

The band took a seven-month break after that series of tours and began trying out new songs: "Lucia Got Deported Last Night"; "Somewhere, Sometime, We'll Be Okay"; "Siobhan's Holding Again"; "The Shooting at the Playhouse Lounge"; "Leticia & Yolanda"; "Now He's Walking with His Sleeves Down"; "Holly's at the Checkout with a Half Gallon of Vodka and a

Pack of Diapers"; "My Whole Life I've Just Been Knocking Around"; "The Coyote Rip-off"; "Dilaudid Diane"; "The Security Guard"; "Manny Got Killed Last Night"; "Why Do We Have to Spend Our Whole Lives Just Scraping By?"

They added a monthlong tour before recording the new record, and the brothers seemed better. Lou had a girlfriend in Reno named Rachel Ortega, who was in college studying to be an elementary school teacher. He told the band he was in love with her. On the road he began waking up early to talk to her before she went to school. One morning as they checked out of a motel, he even came to the van with a dozen donuts and four coffees. They got on the interstate and ate the donuts and Lou told the guys he was going to marry her. "I mean I just had phone sex with her in a fucking phone booth at nine a.m. I mean she's smart, she's gonna be a teacher like Ma, but she's wild. Wild and straight at the same time. What else could you ask for?" And when he got done telling the band, Jaime just laughed and ate the donuts and drank the coffee. No biting comments were said. He just seemed happy for his brother.

Lou spent the tour walking around with a sock full of quarters and he'd call his girlfriend every chance he could. He partied but not in the way he had on previous tours, and when Al suggested he take a night off, he took a night off. Jaime didn't seem jealous; more than anything, Lou falling in love just seemed to make him step back from all of them a little. He spoke less around the band and began going off by himself when they had free time on the road.

The last five dates of that tour they opened for an East Coast band. They played a club in Philadelphia and got a hotel down the street from the venue. The van was secured in a locked garage and they had a short drive the next day to Baltimore. After the gig the brothers left with a group of people from the headlining band, and Bic and Al went back to the hotel and drank beer, ate takeout Chinese food, and watched TV.

It wasn't yet dawn when they were woken by a pale and sick-looking Lou. He stood in the doorway with tears leaking down his face. Jaime had gone back to the woman from the headlining band's hotel room. She was a known junkie and she and Jaime shot heroin. They both nodded out but Jaime, who wasn't used to heroin, overdosed and died in her room.

Lou, Bic, and Al sat in the hotel for what seemed like hours and then Lou left to call his mother. Al did the business of the band. He told the record label and booking agent and let the front desk know they were staying another night. That evening Al and Bic picked up Mrs. Sanchez at the airport and drove her to the hotel. Lou couldn't get out of bed until his mother arrived and then got up only to fall into her arms.

They arranged to have Jaime's body flown back to Reno and that next afternoon they drove Lou and Mrs. Sanchez to the airport. From there Al and Bic drove the van three days straight and arrived in Reno at five in the morning and parked in front of Bic's mom's house and unloaded his gear. Bic said he hoped that someday he and Al could start another band together. "You been the best friend I ever had," he said. "You won't forget me, will you?"

"No, I won't forget you," Al said. "I could never forget you."

Al drove the van to the duplex and unloaded his gear. Inside he saw that his TV, his entire record collection, his stereo, and all of Colleen's things were gone. On the refrigerator was a three-line note saying she was moving to Las Vegas and that she'd get ahold of him as soon as she could. In a panic he ran down to the basement to find his two Fender Deluxe amps, a 1969 SG, his Martin acoustic, and a 1971 Gibson ES-335 still there.

That afternoon he drove the van to the brothers' house and parked. He unhooked the battery, put the keys through the mail slot of the mother's house, and walked to the Cal Neva and ordered a Denver omelet, a beer, and a Hornitos on the rocks. After that he bought a six-pack and a fifth of Centenario and walked home. He didn't get out of bed for three days and then went on a monthlong bender and came out of it so shaky and sick that he drove down to Mel and the mining claim to once again dry out.

16

Al's legs began to shake again and he collapsed in the middle of the road. Behind him storm clouds made their way through the mountains toward the foothills. His right leg cramped and he gasped in pain. He straightened it slowly and tried to breathe as he looked out at the beauty of the valley. Even as a boy he had loved it there, the isolation and peace and grandness of it. If he couldn't go on, if he died in the middle of the road, froze to death, maybe that wouldn't be the worst thing. Maybe walking to save the horse was all that he had in him. Maybe, in the end, he was only strong enough for that. He lay on his back in the snow and gave in to the cold and weariness. He fell asleep.

"I had a dream last night and in my dream the darkness kept pulling me farther out. I was so scared I didn't know what to do. I know I talk a big game but I didn't want to be out that far. It was awful. There was just nothing in any direction but darkness. I began to drown. I'd finally done it. I wasn't strong enough to get back . . . At first I didn't give up. For a long time I really did try, but after a while, well . . . I couldn't try anymore and I quit using my arms and then after a while I quit using my legs and I sank and sank and everything went black and silent. The next thing I know I'm back in Reno walking down Virginia Street and it's winter and snowing and I'm freezing. I was so cold that I . . . that I just laid down in a foot of snow in the middle of the road and gave in to it. I was so

sad, Al. I was so . . . And then I heard the sound of somebody walk-
ing and an old bag lady knelt down beside me and she said, 'Don't
worry, Maxine. You're okay now.' She held my hand, and her hand
was so warm. It was so soft and gentle and she was so nice and her
voice was so beautiful. Her name was Helen, and she told me this
thing, Al. She told me that all the sad and ruined people were living
on this one street. And they were all okay there, they were all free
from themselves, free from their pain and their heartache. I didn't
understand what she was saying because there was nothing around
us. All the businesses and houses were boarded up. Not even the
streetlights were working and I couldn't see or hear even a single
car in the distance. Nothing . . . You should have seen her, because
the more I looked at her the more she looked like my grandmother.
She kept hold of my hand and told me that I had to think harder
and disappear harder into myself to find the real street. I know this
all sounds stupid but I tried to do what she said. I tried and tried
and I disappeared into myself as hard as I could and suddenly it
was there. Beauty. I'm serious. Suddenly the street was lit up in old
clubs. They had big neon marquees: the Dutchman's Room, Rudy's
Lounge, the Lost Highway, the Jockey Club, the Pom Pom Room,
Mildred's Marauder Club, Lorna's Place. They were all so beauti-
ful, Al. And I saw Vern in a corner booth kissing Gail Russell and
your uncle Mel and his dogs Sonny and Curly sitting by a coal
fire and my friend Holly was there and Cassie and Annie and
Frank and Jerry Lee and Jimmy the Broom and Jaime and my
aunt Becky and Tito and one-legged Carl and Lefty and Dan.
It went on and on, Al. The streets had old-fashioned Christmas
lights and there was a twenty-piece band playing at a place called
the Primadonna Club. You just have to wake up and then you can
disappear to see it. You'll be safe there. I swear you will be. Because
it's the only way for people like us. People not tough enough to live in

this world. Wake up, Al, please . . . If you wake up, I'll forgive you.
If you wake up, I'll love you again . . . Please, Al . . . Wake up for the
horse. Because the horse has never been given a chance. The horse
has always been pushed around and pushed aside, his whole life he's
been nothing but an afterthought . . . Al!"

Al opened his eyes and looked into a sky that was white. Snow
swirled above him and it was afternoon and windy. He stood
up sore, cold, drunk, and hungover. He took a sip of water and
drank off the tequila bottle and started walking again. One
foot in front of the other. A greater sage-grouse appeared at
the edge of the road, watching him. Its white neck and gray
spiked tail feathers fanned out. It paraded a show and Al
watched until it flew off, disappearing into an endless white
valley.

He thought of Maxine and the dream that woke him and he
thought of Reno and Virginia Street and the diner he'd owned
there. Landrum's Diner. Because he had tried his best to quit
music. He had tried the best he knew how to be normal, to be
like everyone else, and if things hadn't gotten wrecked along
the way, maybe he would have succeeded.

At the time he was thirty-four years old and had been married two years when Maxine's little brother, Harold, came to
the duplex and told them he was trying to buy a diner. The
problem was that he didn't have enough money. He needed a
partner. Landrum's sat on the corner of Arroyo and Virginia
Street and was built to look like an old trailer, painted white
with green trim. Inside were ten stools, a jukebox, a cigarette
machine, and a single employee who cooked, waited on customers, ran the register, did the dishes, and cleaned.

After her brother had left, Al told Maxine he wanted in on it. He explained to her how he was tired of the uncertainty of a musician's life, tired of being gone nearly every night of the week while she sat at home alone. And he was tired of playing other people's songs in casinos. "I mean I play five nights a week with Ronnie Willis, and for what? No one gives a shit, and I never see you. I want to try and live like a normal person. I want to try and be normal." So he put in the eight thousand dollars he had in savings, Harold put in another three, and together with the bank they bought Landrum's. They put in a new floor, bought a modern commercial dishwasher, and Al sold his amps and extra guitars and stored Herb Marks's Telecaster in his basement. He quit writing altogether. And it worked. Al both liked and got along with his brother-in-law, and the only job he'd ever had besides playing guitar was as a cook. He didn't like it, exactly, but he didn't mind it, and he was good at it.

Harold was a short and stubby man with red hair, a drifting left eye, and half a missing pinkie from a deli slicer accident when he was in high school. He could get by on three hours of sleep and woke each morning to put a dip of Copenhagen in his lower lip and a splash of Seagram's in his coffee. He was a good cook who had an encyclopedic memory of jokes, and when Al arrived to work each morning he found Harold had prepped what he was supposed to have prepped, the dishes done, the sugar and salt and pepper shakers and ketchups filled, the floor swept and mopped, and the counters cleaned. It was a good partnership that lasted over three years and only seldom was the place not full. It was a locals' favorite on the upswing. They did a good business and they got along.

Al knew if he could have kept control of his thinking, temper his occasional desire to run out, he could have lived his life working at Landrum's. Because eventually he would have been institutionalized by it and would have grown to accept it as his life. He would have forced the place into his blood, and every afternoon at two p.m. when his shift ended, he would have walked home to Maxine and most likely their kids. It would have been difficult mentally but back then he had the strength to will things. He was almost certain he could have done it without cracking up.

But at the start of his fourth year, he got a call from Lynda Durrell asking him to rejoin their band. A month after that her sister, Lacy, who was in town staying at Harrah's, called Maxine and told her she wanted Al to write songs for them and needed Maxine's help in convincing him to play again. But when Maxine brought it up, Al only shrugged it off. He told her he was through playing music, through with bands, especially casino bands, and was happy with the way things were.

"At least hear what she has to say," Maxine told him. "I mean I think she came all this way just to see you. It would be rude not to at least listen."

So Al went to Harrah's and met Lacy in her hotel room. She answered in jeans and a purple blouse. She wore silver hoop earrings and her fingernails were painted black. Al stood near the TV and Lacy sat on the edge of the bed and told Al that Lynda & Lacy were making a permanent move to Las Vegas. They had landed a six-month stint at the Sands and had signed a recording contract with a label out of Los Angeles due, in large part, to his song "Sad-eyed Black-and-Blue Sue."

"Lynda's in Vegas right now finding us an apartment. I came here because I wanted to tell you some things. We're always looking for songs, not just the hits we have to play but real songs. Songs that mean something to us. It's the only way we'll ever break out of the casino circuit. We have to have our own, well . . . personality, maybe. Our own style. Lynda and I are always arguing about it. The thing is, the only time we don't argue is when it comes to your songs. I know you've gotten married and moved on, but I want you to know that the way you wrote for us, I feel those songs and Lynda still feels them, too. And we miss the way the band sounded with your guitar. I know it's been years, but we were a real band when you were with us. Now we're just another stupid lounge act. But the thing is, Al, we're starting to do good and we've gotten better. We really have . . . What I'm saying is, without you, I don't think us making a record will make a difference. But with you it will. Continuity and all that, vision, an identity of our own. With you I think we could be big-time. Lynda feels the same way. We really want to make it, Al. We have to make it. So will you come back?"

Lacy was tall and thin, a singer who looked like a fashion model. She was the star of the sisters and the reason they got work. It wasn't just that she was beautiful, she could sing. Her voice cracked when it should crack and held when it should hold. She was always on key, said funny things between songs, and never forgot lyrics.

"I can't."

"Why?"

"I own the diner and I don't want to be away from my wife."

"Bring her with you."

"Thanks, but no."

Al could see Lacy trying to think. After a time she said, "You know, even though it's been five years, we still play your songs: 'Sad-eyed Black-and-Blue Sue'; 'A Bus Ticket to Houston'; 'Lately I've Been Going Down'; and 'Long Hauling, Long Hurting, Long Overdue.'"

Al shook his head. "The only one that might be any good is 'Lately I've Been Going Down.'"

"You're wrong. They're all good. Lynda and I both think so. That's why I'm here and that's why I checked with Maxine first. I want everything to be right. She told me she wants you to start playing again. She really loves your songs, too. So please, Al, at least sit down. Lynda and I got you some presents and you have to get those before you leave." She pointed to a table and chairs and he sat. From a paper sack she took a fifth of Centenario tequila. She put it on the table, took two glasses from the dresser, poured each of them a drink, and sat across from him. "Have you ever had real tequila?"

"I don't think so. But I don't drink much anymore," he said. "I have a couple beers with dinner but that's about it."

"The married life, huh?"

"Maybe, but I have to leave for work by four-thirty in the morning. That's hard to do drunk or hungover."

"You happy being a cook?"

"Happy enough," he said, and took a sip.

She pointed to the glass. "Do you like it?"

"Sure."

"We've gone through three guitar players since you got hurt, and a few weeks ago our newest one gave notice. We've gone through a drummer and two bass players, too. It's exhausting always having to get everyone up to speed. But things really are starting to go for us. Our guarantees have tripled since you were in the band, and we have a real manager now who handles a lot of the bigger Vegas acts, and he likes

us. So we're in a better financial position and we can offer
you six hundred a week, your own room on the road, and per
diems."

Al finished the drink, moved back in his seat, and shook his
head. "That's a lot of money."

"You're worth it."

"I'm sorry. I really am. I appreciate the offer, I do, but I
can't."

"Will you just write for us, then?"

"I don't think so," he said. "I sold all my stuff. I have my
electric but I keep it in storage in the basement. I haven't written anything in four years. I wouldn't even know where to
start."

"That's why I want to give you your second and third presents. So close your eyes."

"Close my eyes?"

"You'll see."

Lacy went to the closet and took out a guitar case and a spiral notebook and set them on the bed. "Okay, open."

Al saw the guitar case.

"You're too talented not to have a good acoustic guitar."

He walked over to it and took out a 1940 Martin D-28 acoustic. "This is too nice."

"It's not. Will you write me songs on it? Songs that you know
I can sing and believe in."

"I don't know." He sat on the bed and put the guitar on his
lap.

"Please."

He held the guitar without playing it and then put it back in
the case. He looked at the notebook next to it. "You even got
the kind I like."

"I remember some things," she said, and smiled. "So will you?"

"I don't know. I'm in a pretty good place right now."

"You can't be a cook the rest of your life, can you?"

He shrugged and went back to the chair and sat.

She poured him another drink. "Is that any way to live?"

"Is playing casinos? I mean do you even like Las Vegas?"

"We won't be there forever. We're gonna make it, Al. With your help we are. I can feel it."

Al finished the second drink in a swallow and stood. "I appreciate you thinking of me," he said. "But I can't go back to playing and I can't take the guitar. Thanks, but I'm going to go now."

Lacy got up after him. "Will you think it over?"

"I already have."

"At least take the guitar."

"It wouldn't feel right."

"My sister and I bought it for you. You have to take it. Either way he gets the guitar. That's what we agreed."

"I can't."

"You have to. I'm serious. I told Maxine you'd get it."

Al looked at the case on the bed, walked over to it, and picked it up. Lacy took the paper sack off the dresser, put in the tequila and the notebook, and handed it to him. "You're sure walking that rope, aren't you, Al?"

"I'm trying," he said.

But within weeks of that meeting, Maxine's mother had broken her foot. The break was complicated by diabetes. She couldn't work and had to have surgery and a halo put around her foot and ankle. The foot had to be elevated for three months. She couldn't walk, was confined to a wheelchair, and needed a caregiver. So Maxine, who already had a troubled relationship with her mother, quit her job to do it.

Looking back on it, Al knew it was all a test. The hard times testing the easy, and of course he had failed the test. He had failed because in his heart he didn't want to be a cook in a diner for the rest of his life. He didn't want to get up at four a.m. and work and talk to customers all day and come home exhausted, smelling of grease. The same thing over and over day after day and month after month and year after year.

Even before the meeting with Lacy, Al had begun to struggle. He had bought a notebook and was secretly writing lyrics before the diner opened and when his shift was slow. Sometimes on his way home he stopped at the library and sat hidden in an alcove for an hour and worked on lyrics. He didn't even tell Maxine he did this. He was too ashamed.

But the truth was the truth. He was tired of being tired all the time and he dreamed of spending his nights half drunk and he dreamed of sleeping in late and watching afternoon movies and working on songs. The sisters' offer was six hundred dollars a week. It was twice what he made at the diner and it was easier work. It was nothing compared to the alarm going off and being on your feet all day standing over a grill.

Each day Maxine drove to her mother's apartment and took care of her. She shopped for her, bathed her, cleaned, and cooked her meals. So when Al finally told her he was thinking of taking the Durrell sisters' offer, she sobbed in relief. They could move to Las Vegas, she said, and she could find a job she liked and finally get away from Reno and her mother. They could rent the duplex out. They could live the easy life for a while. She told Al that she had been dreaming of them leaving and never coming back. "I'll get my mom settled and I'll meet you down there," Maxine said. "We'll escape. Some people get to escape, and we'll be those people."

So Al took the job. He sold his share of the diner to Harold and took a bus to Las Vegas with two guitars, an amp he'd just purchased, and a suitcase of clothes.

17

In Vegas Al practiced night and day to get his chops back and get up to speed with the band's songs and arrangements. The gig was four sets a night, six nights a week, and every gig was the same, on the same stage, on the same casino floor. They played to drinkers and gamblers and tourists. When each night finished, Al didn't drink or stay out. He went back to his room and tried to write songs. In the mornings he ate breakfast, took a daily walk, and went back to his room and kept at it. The only breaks he gave himself were movies. Four times a week he'd walk to a theater and see a matinee, and every payday he sent all but fifty dollars home.

But the first month passed, as did the second, and Maxine didn't come to Las Vegas. Her mother's foot wasn't healing the way they had hoped and the doctor had scheduled an amputation. Al flew home twice on his single night off to find Maxine in trouble. She was struggling to get out of bed. Adding to it was her brother, Harold. He was no longer speaking to their mother. They'd had a fight that ended so badly, he refused to help in any way. So Maxine was alone. On one of his nights home, Al went to his mother-in-law and told her he would rent them a house in Las Vegas where they could all live together. But she refused to move.

After the fourth month, Al decided to quit the band and return home when the six-month stint at the Sands ended. He met with the sisters, explained the situation, and played them the songs he'd written. "Laid Up in a Las Vegas Lounge"; "Every Time I Say Your Name I Get Blue"; "Crying from a Pay Phone"; "Sammy, Lucky & Me"; "Are You Thinking About Somebody New?"; "Elroy and Tuscaloosa Sal"; "Wasted in a Holiday Inn"; "Bonnie and Me"; "Can You Get Me Out of Phoenix?"; "Layover in Tokyo"; "High Time We Quit This Low Living." The two sisters listened, took note of the ones they liked, and scheduled a day at a local studio for Al to record demos.

A week after that he wrote a song called "The Night Ain't Meant for Me." He didn't know what to think of the tune but the sisters were ecstatic over it. The band learned it in one rehearsal, and from the first time performing it, they could all feel the song was different; the crowd's reaction was different. It was the song, the sisters said, that they had been waiting for Al to write.

The first night after they had played it live, a knock came on his hotel room door at one in the morning. He opened it to see Lacy in front of him dressed in a black silk robe and carrying a bottle of Centenario. "I got you a gift," she said, and handed him it.

"What for?"

"'The Night Ain't Meant for Me.' It's such a great song, Al. I knew you'd write one like that. I just knew it. Will you have a drink with me?"

Al stepped back and Lacy walked in. Against the wall was the Martin guitar and on a table that overlooked the lights of the Strip was a half-eaten turkey sandwich, two bottles of beer sitting in an ice bucket, and an open notebook. Lacy stopped in front of two photos of Maxine taped to a mirror above the dresser. One was of her sitting on the back steps of the duplex in shorts and a T-shirt. She wore sunglasses and was smiling. A blue bandanna held her hair back. The other was of her in San Francisco's Chinatown. She had her arm around a statue of a dragon and was kissing its face.

"You must miss your wife bad, huh?"

"I do," Al said, and took two glasses from the dresser, opened the bottle, and poured each of them a drink. "You're staying at the hotel tonight?"

"Yeah. I had a voucher for a suite and I didn't feel like going home," she said, still looking at the photos. "Is all you do here at night is write songs?"

"I walk around sometimes."

"Don't you get bored?"

"Not really."

"Every night the same thing?"

Al nodded and handed her a drink.

"And the days?"

"I see movies and I've been jogging."

"Jogging?"

"I'm trying to get in better shape."

"You get lonely?"

"Sometimes."

"Can I ask you a question?"

"Sure."

"If you're so in love, why do you always look so sad?" She took a drink and turned to him. "Are you always sad, Al?"

"I don't know," he said, and smiled. "Sometimes I don't think so, but then other times . . ."

"And why are all your songs sad? Every single one of them."

He shrugged. "They've always been that way. Even when I was a kid, I wrote them like that. I don't know why exactly, but that's the way they come out."

Lacy sat on the bed and Al went back to his chair by the desk. He looked at her bare legs where a thick red scar ran up the side of her right calf and twisted up her thigh and disappeared into the robe. She saw him looking at it. "I got it a couple years ago. I was heartbroken over this guy who wouldn't marry me and I got stupid one night and rolled my car. But that's all in the past. I have a new boyfriend now and he's dying to marry me and owns three car dealerships."

"Congratulations."

"It would be if I liked him," she said, and laughed.

She poured another drink and walked to the window. She looked out over the Vegas Strip. When she turned around, her robe was open. She didn't say anything, she only walked to where Al sat. She moved within a foot of him and grabbed his hand and put it between her legs. And that was all it took.

They stumbled to bed that night and again the next. But the second night Al woke in a cold sweat at three a.m. and thought he was going to be sick. He got out of bed but couldn't catch his breath. He woke Lacy and told her he couldn't sleep with her anymore. He walked bent over as though he had been stabbed in the stomach. He began crying. "I'm sorry, I really am. I really like you but I love my wife and I can't lose her."

Lacy didn't seem upset when he said it. She sat up in bed and listened and agreed. It had been a stupid idea. He was married, he wanted to stay with his wife, she had a boyfriend who wanted to marry her, and they worked together. It was smart, she told him, to stop it before it really began.

So they did. The week after, it was like nothing had happened. Lacy treated Al as she always had. A month passed and it was the same. By then the band had only three weeks left in the residency and Al had nearly forgotten about their nights together. And then Lacy came to the gig one evening and announced to everyone that she had eloped with her car dealership boyfriend, and after that she began coming to the gigs drunk and out of sorts. She forgot lyrics and berated the crowd for not listening. She argued with her sister onstage and complained about the band.

They had scheduled a recording session after the Sands engagement and Al agreed to it as his last commitment. He kept to himself, played the nightly gig, and went back to his room and continued to try and write the sisters songs: "Wrecking Every Marriage on Our Street"; "The Girl with Drowning Eyes"; "Whiskey Saturday, Suicide Sunday"; "What We Ruin We Can't Also Save"; "The Biloxi Blowup"; "The Woman Who Disappeared."

The Sands residency ended. Al had five days off before the recording session and flew home to find Maxine in worse shape. She was in the middle of a full-blown depression. Her days and nights were spent caring for her mother, and her brother, Harold, still wouldn't help. The doctors had amputated her mother's foot and Maxine was trying to get the state to help pay for a daytime nurse and to get her mother put on disability. On the drive home from the airport Maxine pulled the car over to the side of the road. "I'm just so glad you're here," she said, sobbing. "I've been counting the days. I know that sounds lame but I really have been. I've been dying for you to come home. I'm sorry to be so dramatic but . . . I mean I wanted to act happy for you and celebrate but I just don't think I can. I feel like I'm . . . I feel like I'm suffocating, Al . . . I'm . . . I haven't felt this way in so long . . . And my mom is being so mean and my brother won't help and I . . . . I've just been feeling so trapped and hopeless and alone. Lately I haven't been able to see the point of anything, you know? But now you're here and it's like I'm saved again."

The casino band wasn't invited to the recording session. Only the manager, Al, and the sisters came. The producer used a studio band with Al on rhythm guitar and they cut ten of Al's tunes for a session of fifteen tracks. When they finished the basics, everyone seemed happy with Al's songs and the session in general. The producer told Al his part was done. They celebrated at a Chinese restaurant in Hollywood and it was there that Al thanked the sisters and their manager. He told them he would write them songs from Reno but he was now officially out of the band.

"We kept hoping you'd change your mind after the recording," Lynda said. "Are you sure?"

"I'm sorry, but I gotta get home."

Lacy slumped down in her seat and quit talking. Lynda and the manager, who were now dating, asked if Al would do a week of outdoor shows in Vegas before he went home, and he said he would. The gigs were corporate parties and trade-show events. The money was good and the shows were easy, and when the band finished those, they had a small going-away party for Al at Lynda's apartment. A banner was put up that said *We Love You Al!*, and they had a cake and food delivered. It was an afternoon party and nearly over when Lacy and her car dealership husband arrived. Lacy was drunk and red-faced from crying and her husband, who was dressed in white pants, huaraches, and a Hawaiian shirt, walked over to where Al stood in the kitchen and, without saying a word, began punching him on the side of the head.

Three ribs were cracked and his cheek was fractured. From the hospital he called Maxine at her mother's apartment to tell her what had happened to find she already knew. Lacy had called the duplex. "The strange thing is that I hadn't been there in a week," Maxine said. "I was just getting an old coat of mine and the phone rang." Lacy told Maxine about the affair. She said she wanted to punish Al for leaving the band when they were on the verge of making it and she wanted to punish Maxine for marrying him and causing the whole thing to be ruined in the first place.

"'Fuck you' was the last thing she said to me, Al, and then she just hung up."

18

Dusk came and Al looked through his backpack to find he'd forgotten his headlamp and flashlight. With clouds covering the sky and no moon, he couldn't walk at night without them. He kept on until he came to a queen-size box spring, a half-dozen filled industrial-size garbage bags, and an old dresser that someone had dumped by the side of the road. He decided to stay the night there.

In near-darkness he broke up the wood from the box spring and dresser and shook snow from surrounding sagebrush until he found a dead one and tore off pieces from it. He looked through the trash bags for paper and cleared the ground of snow and dug a small pit. He lit a Frosted Flakes cereal box and surrounded it with small pieces of wood. After three false starts, the fire took.

He drank sips off the tequila bottle and nursed the flames. In the distance he heard the yips of coyotes but could see nothing beyond the light of the small fire. He fell asleep. When he woke, the fire was out and he was shivering cold. He was in complete darkness and there was no sound in the valley. His first thought was of the horse alone and blind and freezing. He began to weep and used his lighter to see and added paper from the garbage bags and small pieces of wood from the dresser and mattress frame. The flames again took and he rebuilt the fire.

He thought of a ballad he'd written called "Sitting on the

Curb Watching Our House Burn Down." The song was the story of his divorce from Maxine. Even after all the years that had passed, he had never forgotten the day the Greyhound bus arrived at the Reno station and how he took a taxi to the duplex with his guitars, amp, and suitcase. His ribs taped, his face black and blue and swollen. He was so sore that he had to pay the taxi driver to carry his things from the cab to the front steps.

Inside, Maxine couldn't look at him. She sat at the kitchen table and broke down sobbing. She kept her eyes closed and was nearly hyperventilating when she spoke. She told Al she was going to continue living with her mother, but even so she wanted him to sleep in the basement if he planned to stay there at all. He wasn't allowed in their bedroom anymore and she had already moved his clothes and personal things down there. Al tried to explain what had happened, why he'd done what he'd done, but nothing he said made a difference.

He slept in the basement on the twin bed he grew up on. Seldom did he see Maxine and when he did, he begged, day after day, for another chance. He told her he'd do whatever she said to make amends. He would jump through any hoop she had, he just needed her to give him a hoop to jump through. But no matter what he said or how he said it, Maxine's depression and anger and distrust never wavered.

And then she came to the duplex one morning and told Al that she did forgive him, that she still loved him, but she would never again trust him and because of that she wanted a divorce. "What's the point of anything if I can't trust you? You're supposed to be my best friend. But what I've realized is that I don't have my best friend anymore, because how can you not trust your best friend? So what I have is nothing and all you do is remind me of that." She looked so rough and tired and sick and said it with such heartbroken acceptance that Al didn't fight. He quit begging and quit calling her at her mother's apartment. He packed his things and got a weekly room at the Stardust Lodge Motel and left her alone. Maxine filed for divorce and moved in with her mother and Al moved back to the duplex. When his ribs healed, he got the job as a breakfast cook at Little Sam's Restaurant and Bar.

19

There were still embers in the firepit when Al woke again. His hands and feet were numb and he was sore and hungover and drunk. In one of the trash bags he found pieces of cardboard and part of a magazine and built up the flames again. His watch said five a.m. He took a sip off the tequila bottle and walked circles around the small fire until it was light.

The road in front of him was flat and wide and covered in snow. The sky was cloudless and growing blue. He had survived the night. He put the fire out and began walking. A frozen wind came from the west and a small herd of antelope appeared at the edge of the distant foothills and he saw two lone mallards fly low across the valley. He took sips off the tequila until the bottle was empty.

An hour passed and he saw three wild horses half a mile ahead of him. He thought of the times when he had driven the Monte Carlo down to the flats to jog in running shoes and sweats that he'd bought in Las Vegas. He'd see wild horses, antelope and deer, coyotes, and once even a dying cow. There were other times, early on, when he would put a pack together and walk for hours. He'd hike through the Toiyabe Range or the Shoshone Mountains and camp.

He opened a can of Campbell's beef with vegetables and barley soup. He dumped out half and added water from his bottle, stirred it with a spoon, and ate what he could before continuing on. A tune called "That's Just the Way It Goes, Cowboy" came to him and he began humming it.

He'd been forty-seven when he wrote it and he'd written it because a man came into Little Sam's one afternoon and asked the bartender if he knew Al Ward. The bartender pointed to the cook and said, "That's him over there behind the grill." The man, Larry Hillson, lived in Nashville and was in Reno as a road manager for a band called Cowboy Pride performing two nights at the Nugget Casino.

When Al finished his shift, the two sat at the bar and Larry told him he had been a fan of The Sanchez Brothers when he was in college. He'd flown out two days early to track down Lou Sanchez, who was now living in Gardnerville and owned a concrete-cutting business. Lou explained to Larry that even though the writing credits were given to Lou, Jaime, Wayne, and Al, they hadn't written any of the songs. Only Al had.

"Is that true?" Larry asked.

"I guess so," Al said. "But a lot of the lines were stuff the brothers would talk about. Mostly I just listened and took notes. How did Lou seem?"

"Good. He's married."

"To Rachel?"

"Yeah. They have a kid, around four or five, a boy named Jaime. Lou's a lot heavier than he looks on the record covers."

"Lou's fat?"

"Nah, but he's filled out."

"That's good," Al said. "That's a relief to hear. Back in the day the brothers never ate. They'd stay up for days on end, and . . . So he's okay?"

"Yeah."

"I haven't seen him in a long time. It was just too hard after Jaime. We tried, but . . ."

Al fell silent and drank his beer and Larry cleared his throat and sang in an out-of-tune voice.

Marianne, Marianne, Marianne's in the mental ward
Looking out at Glendale she don't sleep no more
Shaky hands and shaky eyes
So full of pills she can't cry
I miss her so bad I don't know what to do
But Marianne ain't getting out anytime soon
Marianne, Marianne, Marianne's in the mental ward
She tried to hang herself with an extension cord

Al shook his head and laughed.

"That's always been one of my favorites. This morning I listened to it while I drove by the mental hospital on Glendale. Was Marianne real?"

"She was a woman I hung out with for a while," Al said.

"What happened to her?"

"I don't know. I was only with her a few months and that was years ago . . . She was too much for me. It just took me a bit before I could see how off she was, you know? She was so beautiful you couldn't help but get sidetracked. But she wouldn't take her meds and . . . It was maybe six months after I quit seeing her that she was put in there. I don't know what got her committed but I heard it took her a year to get out. After that she was supposed to move to Santa Cruz and live with her grandmother but she never showed up. Her sister put her on a bus, but Marianne missed her transfer in Sacramento."

"You think she's still alive?"

"Man, I just don't know. I hope so."

Larry took a drink of beer. "The reason I've tracked you down is that I'm always looking for songs. Not as fast and raw as The Sanchez Brothers, but if you slowed those down and cleaned up some of the lyrics, they're really great. You still writing?"

"Sometimes."

"You have any that might fit the bill?"

"I don't know."

"Can I ask you another question?"

"Sure."

"Why didn't you ever leave Reno after The Sanchez Brothers? I mean, no offense, but this place is fucking depressing and there's nothing I can see going on music-wise. Why didn't you move to Nashville or at least LA? I bet you could have done something in either place."

"I don't know," Al said. "I guess I just always liked it here. And my ex-wife lives here." He paused and tried to smile. "And shit, man, the truth is I just don't think I ever had the guts to move. My nerves probably would have given out if I had, and I can't afford that."

Larry finished his beer and took a card from his shirt pocket and handed it to Al. "Send me some songs if you want. I might be able to find them homes and get you some money."

"Thanks."

"And if you ever get to Nashville, look me up."

"Okay."

"Can I ask you one more question?"

"Sure."

"What about 'Slow Down, Salvador Sánchez, Slow Down'? That guy was a hell of a boxer."

"I guess he was," Al said. "I don't know much about boxing but the brothers loved him and told people they were related to him although I don't think they were. They wanted me to write a tune about him so I did. I went to the library and researched him. Salvador Sánchez liked to drive fast and that's how he died, wrecked his sports car. So that's where I got the lyrics. Plus the brothers always had to play fast. They were always trying to go faster and faster and sing as many words as they could as quick as they could. So that tune just made sense."

Al bought records by the artists Larry Hillson had talked about and tried to write songs he thought might fit on one of those records. More than anything, he supposed, it was a project to focus on and a reason to keep himself in check. At the time he was playing every Thursday, Friday, and Saturday night with Ronnie Willis and Sunday nights with a sixty-year-old lounge singer named Diane Price.

On his nights home he limited himself to two beers and for over eight months did nothing but work, do his gigs, watch TV, make recipes from Italian cookbooks, and write songs. He sent Larry eight tunes that were half modern country/half throwbacks to classic country, songs he thought could be singles. "Wasted in Wichita"; "I'll Take the Slow Boat"; "I Can't Turn Back the Darkness"; "That's Just the Way It Goes, Cowboy"; "When the Mascara Runs"; "Riding the Neon Lights Down to the Bottom"; "Every Woman in Every Car"; "A Girl Left Crying on a Dead-end Street." He recorded them on a battery-powered portable cassette deck and sent them along with the lyrics to the address on Larry Hillson's card.

Ten days later he received a call at Little Sam's. Larry wanted three of them: "That's Just the Way It Goes, Cowboy"; "When the Mascara Runs"; and "I'll Take the Slow Boat." He said he'd give Al five thousand dollars for the rights. Al lied and told him he'd just sent the songs to a half-dozen other publishers and he'd have to wait and see what they said. Larry paused and said he'd give Al six thousand cash for "That's Just the Way It Goes, Cowboy." "But if I buy it, I get the publishing," he said.

"I figured you would."

"You'll get your cut from BMI or whoever you use. And your name will be on it."

"For six grand I'll do that," Al said, and after work that day he went to a notary and wrote out what Larry wanted. Larry received it and wired Al the six thousand dollars. Three weeks later he bought both "When the Mascara Runs" and "I'll Take the Slow Boat" under the same conditions for three thousand.

It was a year after that when Al heard "That's Just the Way It Goes, Cowboy" on a country radio station. He was doing the morning prep at Little Sam's when the song came on, sung by a guy named Tommy Smoke. The singer had a classic country voice and the arrangement was nearly the same as the rough recording Al had done on the portable cassette player. He drank a cup of coffee and turned up the kitchen radio. In total he heard the song five times over the course of a month and for one week it made it to number ninety-three on the national country chart. Al called Larry to thank him but the secretary who answered the phone said Larry no longer worked at the company. She didn't have forwarding information and he never heard from Larry Hillson again.

Al turned fifty-one in 1996. It was the year when alcohol began to catch him. He slurred when in the past he had never slurred. More often he vomited and he spent longer periods on the toilet. He also began to pass out. Twice at a bar called the Lost Highway, once in the back of the Elbow Room, and one morning he woke up at dawn with no recollection of why he was sitting on the dirt outside of Mountain Vistas Mobile Home Park.

Al mentioned what was happening to an old man named R.J. who sat at Little Sam's each morning and drank Jameson on ice. R.J. was bald and thin and five feet seven inches tall. For forty years he had been married to a onetime showgirl who was six-two at her tallest. When the restaurant was slow, Al would sit beside him at the bar and drink coffee. "I'm just telling you the truth, Al," R.J. said. "Nothing good happens in a bar at night to a guy over fifty. It's just a fact. So if you're gonna drink out, drink during the day, because day drinking is old-man drinking. And if you can't figure out how to do that financially or with your family then don't drink. I'm telling you, man, be home by sunset with your door bolt locked and your slippers on. It's the only way."

Al tried to follow the advice. He quit seeing bands and bar-hopping and he stopped playing drunken slots and eating late-night meals at casinos. He tried to stay home. He bought a VCR and rented movies. He collected 1930s jazz records and Morricone soundtracks, and even though he had no one to write for, he obsessively worked on a series of folk ballads.

"The Oil Rig Fire," "A Girl from New Orleans," "The Tijuana Killings," "The Ballad of Jaime Sanchez," "Colleen Where Are You Now?," "Polly OD'd Last Night," "The Cops at the El Cortez," "The Motorcycle," "Blue to Blackout," "The Missing Girl," "Pickpocket Pauline," "The Ballad of Helen Casey," "The Handicapper," "No Sleep Lorna," "The Fight at the Turf Club,"

"The Kid They Found by the Tracks," "The $15,000 Streak," "The Short-Order Cook," "The Rundown," "She Grew Up on the Gulf of Texas," "Billy and Lorraine," "The House Robbers," "Sitting in the Movies Alone," "The Marauder," "Makeshift Living Ain't No Living at All," "A Burning Car on the Flats," "The Beating Outside the Ponderosa Casino," "Gail the Grifter," "The Back Room of the St. Francis Hotel," "Cowboy Jim and the Narcoleptic."

When he was done with those, two years had passed. He bought a harmonium and began writing story songs with slow, brooding melodies, the shortest being just under nine minutes.

"The Killing of a Motel Maid," "A Drink Before Work," "Waking Up Outside of Bruno's," "The Le Mans," "Waiting for You to Get Off Work," "I Hope You Don't Ever Have to See Me This Way," "Nancy and the Pensacola Pimp," "The Used-Car Lot," "Little Leon and Josie the Junkie," "Blood on the Kitchen Floor," "Let Me Sleep Until My Fight's Over," "The Holdup," "Darkness Is the Only Friend I've Always Had," "The Ballad of Frank and Jerry Lee."

20

If he would have started the Monte Carlo more often, kept the batteries charged, or bought a four-wheeler like Lonnie had advised, then none of it would be as bad as it had become. The coyotes wouldn't have found the horse and he wouldn't have had to kill the one he had. He wouldn't have started drinking. He would have just woken up, seen the blind horse, and gotten into his car and driven to Morton's for help. But because he was the way he was, the horse was now most likely dead, he himself was drunk, and no matter how hard he tried, he couldn't stop thinking of things he didn't want to think about. Even hiding out on the claim, away from everything and everyone, he had caused pain to others and his past had continued to haunt him.

In the distance Morton's ranch sat at the foothills of the Hot Creek Range. A half-dozen horses stood in a snow-covered field below a white Craftsman house where a trail of chimney smoke rose. A red hay barn sat to the right of it, a smaller equipment barn behind it, and on the outskirts of the property, farthest from the road, stood a white cinder-block bunkhouse. As Al got closer he began jogging, and by the time he was to the house and knocking on the oak front door he could barely stand.

Dogs barked from inside and the door opened and Georgie, Lonnie's black-and-white border collie, came out wagging the nub of her tail. Behind her was another black-and-white border collie, skinny and younger, who let out a single weak howl. In the doorway stood a young blond woman dressed in gray University of Arizona sweats and black slippers.

"Are you Al?" she asked.

Al nodded but couldn't catch his breath.

The woman smiled. "Are you okay?"

Al shook his head.

"Why don't you come inside. I was making coffee when I saw you coming up the road. Lonnie was asleep but I woke him and he got the binoculars and said it might be you. He's just putting on his clothes."

Al's face was red and his hands were covered in dirt and ash and charcoal. He smelled of smoke and tequila. "Lonnie's here?" he whispered, and tears welled in his eyes.

"Yeah, he's here. I'll get him." The woman walked down the hall and trotted up the stairs. The floor was oak and the living room was empty but for a woodstove burning. Along the back wall were a stack of boxes and a new sectional couch wrapped in plastic. Al stood next to the woodstove and Lonnie came from the hallway limping, his right knee buckling as he went.

"Al!" he cried. He was dressed in jeans, a flannel shirt, and wool slippers. He smiled when he shook Al's hand. "Shit, you look like a mountain man and if I ain't mistaken, you're as drunk as a monkey. What, did you walk all the way here?"

Al nodded.

"Car wouldn't start, huh?"

He shook his head.

"That's thirty miles," Lonnie said to the woman. "Something happen, Al?"

Again he nodded and tears streamed down his face.

"Would you like a cup of coffee, Al?" the woman asked.

Lonnie put his arm around her. "Al, this is Sammi. I met

her in Arizona. She's the best, man. You want a beer with your coffee?"

Al nodded and they went to the kitchen and he sat at a long wooden table with bench seats. The kitchen cabinets were old, painted white, and the countertops were the same as the floor, faded red linoleum. The sink was white and the stove was electric and avocado-green. A three-foot-wide 1974 Ponderosa Meat calendar hung on the wall, showing a Frederic Remington print of a lone man on horseback riding alongside a stampeding herd of cattle. It had browned with age and was patched in four places with clear tape where it had been torn. To the left of it was an old General Electric clock that said nine-fifteen. Lonnie took a can of Coors from a dented refrigerator, opened the beer, and set it in front of Al. "Drink a little and tell me what's going on."

Al took a long sip but said nothing.

Lonnie sat down across from him. "Did you see the new dog, Tex? Yesterday we were coming back from shopping in Tonopah and we ran into Terrance Johnston. You know him, right?"

Al nodded.

"Well, he was on the side of the road. He'd blown a tire but couldn't change it because his back seized up. He was just standing there bent over. Man, he was in a lot of pain. Tex was sitting in the bed of the truck with a couple other dogs. Terrance was in a shit-ass mood over his back, but also because of Tex. He told us he was gonna shoot him when he got home. Turns out Tex is too meek to herd and has no energy. Terrance said, 'He's six months old, he's scared of everything, and he's like an old man. All he does is shit, sleep, and eat. He ain't no good to me at all.' Sammi pulled me aside and told me we had to save him so I told Terrance I'd change the tire if he'd give me the dog and he agreed. So we took him and I told Sammi that he'd be a good fit for you. You're old, you're scared of everything, and all you do is shit, eat, and sleep." He laughed again. "But we can talk about Tex later."

Al looked at Lonnie and took another sip.

"So that piece-of-shit car of yours didn't start, huh?"

Al shook his head.

"Sammi, he's got this old beater cruiser out at his place. I've told him for years to sell it but he won't. It doesn't even have four-wheel drive." He looked at Al. "And you probably haven't run it once since the last time I saw you."

Al shook his head again.

"Well, that's okay. I'm just sorry I wasn't around. I didn't mean to be gone so long. What about Linden? He checked on you, right?"

Al put up one finger on his right hand.

"Just one time?"

Al nodded.

"That son of a bitch," Lonnie said, and looked at Sammi. "There's this guy who works on a ranch about fifteen miles north of here, Bo Linden. I've never liked him but he's always broke and looking for extra work and he's the only guy I could think of. So I hired him to bring groceries and look after Al while I was gone. I even sent him three hundred of my own dough to make sure he kept going. He promised he'd stop by once a week." Lonnie turned back to Al. "He really only showed up one time?"

Al nodded.

"Man, I'm gonna kill that guy . . . I'm sorry, Al. I didn't know. Well, you're all right now," Lonnie said. "You just gotta tell me what's going on."

Sammi put down three cups of coffee and Al finished the beer. Lonnie took another from the fridge, opened it, and gave it to him. Al took a long drink from the new can and cleared his throat. "There's a horse," he whispered. "An old horse that's standing in front of my house. He's blind and won't eat and I don't know what to do."

"A horse?" Lonnie said, and laughed. "All this is about a horse? You walked thirty miles for a horse?"

"But he's old and blind and coyotes have been after him . . . I didn't know what to do."

"Well, Jesus, I'm relieved," Lonnie said. "I thought you'd killed someone. I really did. I thought maybe you'd finally gone nuts and somebody had come up to your place and was bothering you and you got scared . . . Shit, don't worry about the horse. We'll take care of him. They're a lot tougher than you'd think. When's the last time you ate?"

"I've been eating," Al said.

"You don't look like you've been eating."

"I'll make us some breakfast," Sammi said. "Would you like that, Al?"

Al nodded.

"Good," Lonnie said. "Can I ask you a question?"

"Sure."

"How can you tell the horse is blind?"

"His eyes are swollen shut and there's stuff coming out of one of them."

"Did it look lame?"

Al shrugged.

"Was it standing on all four legs?"

"Yeah."

"Does it have a brand or do you think it's wild?"

"It has a brand."

"Is it male or female?"

"Male, I think."

"Does he have his nuts?"

"I don't know."

"Well, if he doesn't and he has a brand, there's a chance he'll be okay to deal with. I'll go hook up the trailer in case we have to bring him back. You just sit tight and warm up. I'll be back in a few."

Outside the wind howled through the valley and the storm approached. Lonnie hooked his truck to a battered white stock trailer. He grabbed a couple flakes of hay and set them in the bed of the truck. From the bunkhouse he got a twelve-gauge shotgun and a box of shells and put them behind the bench seat. When he came back inside, Sammi was plating scrambled eggs and sausage. Lonnie got out knives and forks and hot sauce and he and Sammi sat across from Al. "Seriously, man," he said, "when was the last time you ate?"

"I had a can of soup on the way here," Al whispered, and took a drink of beer.

"Sammi, one thing to know is Al's a world-class bullshitter. He ain't been eating, because even under his getup and that beard he looks skinny. Even his neck looks skinny. You're wasting away, man."

"You want more coffee, Al?"

Al nodded.

Sammi poured coffee and Lonnie shoveled the breakfast into his mouth. When he finished, he stood up. "Sorry, I always eat fast when I know I have somewhere to be. But you take your time, Al. I'm just gonna put a couple lunches together in case we have to be there a while."

Al nodded and ate a forkful of eggs.

"We're both sure lucky that Sammi cooked. If I was cooking, all you'd get are Pop-Tarts or cornflakes."

"And he'd burn the Pop-Tarts," Sammi said.

"She's right, I probably would."

Lonnie went to the fridge and took a block of cheese and a package of ham and made four sandwiches with mayonnaise, lettuce, and mustard. He wrapped them in wax paper and took out an old red-and-white Playmate cooler from the pantry. He set the sandwiches, a six-pack of beer, and a bag of chips inside the cooler and stood at the edge of the kitchen and watched Al finish his plate. When he had, Lonnie picked up his can of beer. "Miracles happen," he said. "Your plate is empty and the beer is still half full. Looks like we're ready to go."

21

There was a constant limp to Lonnie's gait as he walked down the porch steps in a faded black canvas coat, a stained gray cowboy hat, jeans, and leather boots. In his right hand he held the cooler and he went tentatively across the snow toward the truck. Tex trotted alongside, dipping his nose in and out of the snow, and when Lonnie opened the driver's side door he jumped into the cab. Al got in the passenger side, set his pack on the floor in front of him. Lonnie started the truck and they left the ranch.

At the the main road Al cleared his throat and said, "How did you hurt your leg?"

Lonnie chewed on his fingernails as he drove. "A lot has happened to me since the last time I saw you, Al. And shit, that was only like, what, seven months ago? Last July? It was crazy, man. I got my truck stolen and then I got my knee busted and I ended up in Douglas, Arizona. You know where that is?"

"Not really."

"It's on the border. I was laid out there for a while. But I'll tell you about that some other time. Right now I gotta ask, is there really a horse?"

"Yeah."

"A horse in front of your place?"

"Yeah."

"And it's alive?"

"It was when I left."

"And the coyotes? Were they real?"

Al nodded. "I had to kill one of them."

"With a gun?"

"Yes."

"The rifle you keep in the mine?"

"Yeah."

"And you walked all the way here because of that?"

"Yeah."

"Okay." Lonnie spat out a bit of fingernail. "Can I ask you another question?"

"Of course."

"You ain't gonna be pissed?"

"No."

"Were you drunk when you saw the horse?"

"No. I didn't start drinking until after I saw it. I started drinking because I was gonna shoot it."

"To put it out of its misery?"

"Yeah."

"But you couldn't?"

"No."

Lonnie turned on the radio. "I don't mean to sound like I don't believe you, but you really seem out of sorts. The truth is I've never seen you look this bad. You look like shit, Al."

"I know," Al said. "I look in the mirror. I know what's happening. But the horse is real. It has to be or I don't know anything anymore."

"I hope for your sake it is. Because you seem crazy as shit to me."

Al looked out the window and again was overcome with doubt. He was so tired and drunk and hungover that everything seemed set in a world of haze where he couldn't quite see what was real and what wasn't. He whispered, "I hope it's there."

"And you said it has a brand?"

"On its hip. A big *T* next to a little *t*. It's faded, but that's what it looked like to me."

"I don't know the brand, but if he has one, there's a good chance he might be broke."

"Then how did he get to my place?"

"Who knows. Somebody probably dumped him."

"Abandoned him?"

Lonnie nodded. "It happens more than you think. When Gerry Morton owned the ranch, we caught a guy dumping two horses out near Mine Creek Meadow. That's on his land. We stopped to see what the guy was doing. One of the horses was in the trailer and the other was tied to the side of it. They were both so quiet it was like they'd been in a trailer a thousand times. The guy said they were wild mustangs and he was setting them free. But they had shoes on and were both gelded. They weren't wild mustangs." Lonnie let out a bitter laugh and leaned into the steering wheel. "They were just old useless quarter horses, that's what they were. Gerry wanted to shoot the guy. You can say what you will about Gerry, but he loves horses."

"I miss Gerry."

"I'm sure you do."

"I still don't understand why he sold the ranch."

"Well," Lonnie said, "he doesn't have kids and none of his cousins want to take it over. And shit, he's old like you. He wants to live in Mexico and try to get a new wife. That's hard to do out here. So I guess it's no more of you two staying up all night drinking and keeping everybody on the ranch awake thinking you've seen a UFO." Lonnie looked over to see Al smiling. "You're starting to feel better, huh?"

"A little."

"I got you to smile and now you're petting Tex."

"He's a good dog."

"I wasn't bullshitting. You should take him."

Al quit petting Tex. "I don't deserve a dog."

"You don't deserve it?"

"No."

"Why?"

Flakes of snow began to hit the windshield and Lonnie turned on the wipers.

"I'm not the most reliable."

"Reliable?"

Al nodded.

"Well, I know you brush your teeth because you still have them. And you always shaved, at least you did before I left, and your hair used to look cool, and you always dressed good even though you ain't got a washer and dryer or even running water. You never smell. You're a good cook and you say you got money. You could handle a dog, man. I mean this fella just needs someone to feed him and keep him warm and let him take a leak when he needs to. It's not like you gotta get him into college."

Al put his hand back on Tex. "All right," he said. "I'd love to have him. Thank you."

Lonnie smiled to himself.

"So what happened to those horses?"

"Well, Gerry said if the guy didn't dump them on his place, he'd just dump them somewhere else. So we took them. We named one Shindig and the other Party Man. Joke names because they were both so old and slow. They weren't in the best shape but we had their teeth done, got their weight back up, and after six months I was riding Party Man up into the mountains. The vet thought he was in his mid-twenties. He's a steady little guy that can go and go. Slow as shit but that's the way I like it. Shindig lived another year and then colicked. The vet said he was probably pushing thirty. It was hard on him but he went pretty quick. Party Man was chowing his breakfast this morning. The new owners are letting me keep him and my horse, Jasper. Party Man's a good kid horse, he's bombproof, and they have a couple kids, so I think he'll be all right."

"What are the new owners going to do with the place?"

"They say a vacation home, and they needed a caretaker. I guess when Gerry sold the ranch, he told them about me. And then one night out of the blue the guy called. It was good timing, too. My leg was okay enough to walk on and I could finally get out of Douglas. Besides Sammi, it was the first bit of good luck I had since Gerry sold the ranch. We'll do all right if it lasts."

"I'm glad for you."

Lonnie nodded.

Snow fell harder and the valley disappeared to white. Lonnie could see only fifty feet in front of him. He slowed the truck and turned onto the spur road that went back into the foothills and the mining claim. "Hey, who's singing this one?"

"Freddie Hart," Al said. "It's a tune called 'Easy Loving.'"

"I like this one."

"Yeah, me, too."

"It's starting to come down now."

Al nodded.

"You want to know one more thing about those horses?"

"Sure."

"After the guy took off, Gerry made me walk back to the ranch with them. I was so fucking pissed. He was heading to town to meet some people and didn't want to be late. It was Friday night and I was supposed to tag along to dinner. He said he was gonna buy my chow and all my drinks, too. It was about five miles back to the ranch, so I just started walking them. But I hate walking. After about a mile I came to a rusted-out refrigerator that somebody junked. I tied the lead rope into reins and got on the fridge and jumped on the meekest-looking one, the guy we named Party Man. I rode him the rest of the way home while ponying Shindig."

"You rode him?"

"He was a little saint."

"Why do people do such horrible things?" Al said, and looked out the window.

"They're people, aren't they? . . . Sometimes it seems like people are even worse than you think they could be." Lonnie turned to Al and smiled. "But life ain't all bad. I mean there's Sammi, for instance. She's great, man. She's the first girlfriend I've had in a long time. That's why I gotta apologize for not visiting. We've been back a couple days but we were just getting settled. Testing out the new owner's bed and all that. Plus, I really did think Linden was looking after you."

"I've been all right. Like I said, he stopped by the one time."

"And he brought you food?"

"Three cases of Campbell's soup."

"That's it?" Lonnie said.

Al nodded.

"Was it Chunky Campbell's or the old red-and-white ones? The condensed kind?"

"The old red-and-white ones."

"That son of a bitch. I hate those."

"Me, too."

"So you just been eating that shit for all this time?"

"I had some other stuff for a while."

"Jesus . . . I'm sorry."

"It's not your job to look after me."

"Maybe, but I sorta have been, haven't I?"

"Yeah."

Lonnie kept both hands on the wheel. The truck struggled on the incline and the old stock trailer banged around behind them on the rocks and washouts.

"Al, I gotta tell you something. Is it all right if I do?"

"Of course."

"When I was in Arizona, I was laid up at this place called the Gadsden Hotel. And one day my phone rang. It was a guy named Bobby Winkle. He said he played in a band that came through Tonopah. I can't remember the name of the band but he said you came and saw them. He said afterward you guys played guitars in his motel room. Did that happen? Do you know that guy?"

"Sure, I remember that night."

"Well, Bobby said you left a notebook with your songs in it and he didn't know what to do because he didn't have your phone number or know where you lived. But I guess you put my name and number on the inside cover. So he called me and we got to talking and he said he was worried about you. He said by the end of the night you couldn't keep your story straight. At first you told him you were living with a woman somewhere north of Tonopah on a huge ranch. You said you drove a BMW and had a swimming pool. But by the end of the night you told him you were living in a shack with no electricity. I told him, shit man, that sounds like the Al I know." Lonnie let out a short laugh. "I gotta say, hearing someone else talk about how you are sure made me worry. And me being laid up I couldn't stop thinking, and I came to the conclusion that I'd hung out with you for so long that I'd lost sight of how fucked up you are. No offense."

"None taken."

"I had Bobby send me the notebook and when I got it, I just laid there reading your lyrics. They're so damn good, man. Really. Not that I know anything about anything but I liked them a lot. Bobby said you wrote some of the best songs he'd ever heard. I said old depressed Al did? And he said yeah. Anyway, what I'm trying to get at is toward the back you had a song called 'The Meeting at the Laundromat.' Above it you had written the name Teresa Sanchez and a phone number. You had drawn a heart by her name. Did you write that one about her?"

"Yeah."

"Did you really kiss her by the dryers?"

Al nodded. "It was just a fluke meeting. My washer wasn't working so I was at the laundromat and her dryer broke that same day and she came in with a basket full of wet clothes. It was just luck that we happened to be there at the same time. The place was empty and we . . . we started talking . . . and we couldn't stop talking. We began holding hands and before she left, we kissed. But . . . the thing is, I was in a band with her sons and one of them died. She was just so sad over it all and we just kind of . . ."

"You guys didn't start going out?"

"No," Al said.

"Well, I hope you're not pissed, but one night I phoned her up and she told me about the band you were in with her sons. She said you were really good to them and that she liked you a lot. She told me that a couple times, about how much she liked you. I told her where you were and how you were living and I asked if she could find you a place to live in Reno and she said she had a little house behind her house and you could stay there if you wanted. She told me she wants to help you. At least that's what she said when we were talking. I'm sorry for interfering in your life, Al, but I was all fucked up. I was staying in this weird old hotel and I was broke and my knee was so wrecked I could barely walk. Even the TV in that place didn't work. So I was just stuck there in my head and I guess when you're circling the drain you worry about other people that are, too. She sure has a nice voice on the phone, though. Is she as good-looking as she sounds?"

"Yeah."

"You should date her."

Al laughed. "I'm done with women."

"You should never be done with women."

"You're just in love."

"Maybe, but you should date her anyway. I bet she'd straighten your ass out. And then, shit, Tex showed up and I said to myself, things are looking up for old Al and he doesn't even know it yet. Sammi says I'm a natural matchmaker. Maybe she's right."

"Where did you meet Sammi?"

"In Douglas. But shit, man, she's married."

"Married?"

"They been on the outs for a while but . . . I don't think

she'll go back to him, but who knows. The good news is she's a ranch chick, and her being from Douglas, she thinks this place is lush." Lonnie slowed the truck again and took them down a washout and climbed the other side. He turned the radio up. "Who's singing this one?"

"Freddy Fender. It's called 'Wasted Days and Wasted Nights.'"

"Two songs by guys named Freddy. I like this one a lot. Man, you know every song I ever ask about."

"That's just because this is the only country station we get and they play the same songs year after year. But Freddy Fender was something. I saw him play in Reno in 1977."

"Jesus, I wasn't even born yet," Lonnie said, and slowed the truck to a stop. He pointed out the window. "With all this snow, I'm starting to get nervous about the road. I'm gonna walk up over that ridge. I just want to see what I'm getting into before I get into it." He opened the door and got out. He called for Tex and the dog jumped down off the seat and they disappeared into the falling snow. Al leaned against the door and closed his eyes.

He was sixty years old when he received the call at Little Sam's from Carl Kennedy, his uncle's attorney in Tonopah, that Mel had passed away. Hunters had found his trailer door open and Mel inside, bloated, blue, and dead. The county coroner said Mel had a heart attack and most likely died within the first day of having it. His dog Sonny was gone and never seen again. Al stood behind the bar and listened. "As you know, your uncle made me the executor of his will. I'm calling to let you know he left you everything except his truck and trailer. He gave those to Ricky Lonsdale."

"The old bartender at the Banc Club?"

"You're right. Ricky was that for a while but lately he's fallen on hard times and your uncle knew that."

"I always liked Ricky," Al said, and looked out at the restaurant to see nearly every seat taken. Soon the orders in the kitchen would back up.

"Mel gave you the rest of his assets. The mining claim, everything on the claim, and the thousand acres surrounding it. There are three different parcels in total. He also gave you his savings, which is nearly six hundred thousand dollars in mutual funds."

Tears welled in Al's eyes. "Is he really dead?"

"I'm sorry to be the one to tell you."

"Look, I have to get back to work. It's the lunch rush and I'm the only cook. But I'll drive down tomorrow and see you."

He hadn't been much of a nephew or friend to Mel after he and Maxine split up. Only once during the following years had he gone to visit out of kindness and not desperation. But the one time he had done all right. It was eight months after Lancaster and he took a week off from Little Sam's and left town with a portable CD player, a dozen CDs he thought his uncle would like, and the novels of Alexandre Dumas. In Tonopah he bought his uncle a new Carhartt coat, a pair of long underwear, three pairs of wool socks, and $150 worth of food. He stayed six nights, helped work the claim, and didn't fall apart.

It wasn't much but it was something.

When Mel's estate settled, Al found himself with enough money to live the rest of his life in comfort. Even so he didn't quit his job. He worked at Little Sam's for another two years because he knew if he wasn't forced to get up each morning that most likely he wouldn't get up at all. The money brought him no comfort and he spent none of it.

He wasn't sure whether it was that he no longer had the safety of going to Mel if he fell apart or knowing that he no longer had any family left alive, but Al found himself once again in a sort of slow-motion spiral. His nerves gave out and this time, when he tried to live half drunk, he couldn't. He fell while trying to get up from his chair and broke the headstock off the guitar he was holding. In the middle of the night he got out of bed drunk and tripped going into the bathroom. He hit his head on the toilet, broke the water tank lid, and gashed his cheek. He passed out in Wingfield Park while walking home from a movie. He passed out in the bathtub. He passed out with the stove on, eggs and bacon burning, smoke alarm blaring. He passed out in a booth in the Top Deck restaurant at the Cal Neva and was woken by two security guards.

Looking back on it, he supposed it was the culmination of his body being unable to process alcohol anymore and his mind running out of reasons to keep trying to live that caused him one day to give notice at Little Sam's and put the duplex up for sale. It wasn't that he had a revelation about moving out to the mining claim. It just seemed like the only way he could stop living the way he was living without killing himself. He was sixty-two years old and sold most everything he owned and loaded what he needed into the Monte Carlo and drove south toward Tonopah.

"The bad news is the snow's really starting to dump," Lonnie said when he and Tex got back into the truck. He took his cowboy hat off and shook the snow from it.

"What's the good news?" Al said, and sat up.

"That the road looks all right enough and before too long

I'll be home with Sammi." Lonnie put the transmission in low and started driving again. The truck slid and the tires spun. They nearly got stuck twice but made it through the foothills to the canyon. A half mile into it they came to the mine site, the Monte Carlo, the assayer's office, and standing in the middle of the road, the horse.

"Goddamn, Al," Lonnie said, and let out a laugh. "It is real. I'm sorry, man, but I never would have . . ."

"I wasn't sure either," Al whispered when he saw it, and tears fell down his face.

Lonnie parked the truck and told Al to leave Tex inside the cab and grabbed the rope halter from behind the bench seat and they both got out.

"What's that playing?"

"It's my radio," Al said. "I thought it might scare the coyotes away so I left it on."

"I'll check the horse and you turn it off, okay?"

Al walked over to it, shut it off, and went over to them. Lonnie said it was a gelding and guessed he was twenty years old or more, underweight but not as bad as he could have been. His left hind leg had bite marks on it, part of the hide around the cannon bone was hanging off, but the bleeding had stopped. A few feet behind him was a dead coyote, its muzzle broken in half.

"Looks like the horse got one," Lonnie said, and he put his hand on the horse's neck and the horse didn't scare; didn't seem worried at all. "Ah, hell, Al, he's a little lamb." Lonnie petted him for a long time and then put the rope halter on him. He moved him off the road to the yard in front of the assayer's office and looked at his eyes. "The left one looks shot, all right. There's shit hanging out of it and it's so swollen I don't know if there's even an eye still in there. But the other one might be okay. It just looks full of eye goo. When I put my hand over it, he tries to blink and move his head away. So he has some sorta vision, at least." Lonnie led the horse to where Al stood five feet away. "Hold him for a second."

"What do I do if he runs?"

"He ain't gonna run."

"But what if he does?"

"You really don't know shit about horses, do you?"

"No."

Lonnie laughed and handed Al the halter rope and walked to the truck, took a flake of hay from the bed, and brought it to the horse and held it underneath its nose. He left it there for a minute and the horse began taking bites.

"He's eating!" Al exclaimed.

"That's a good sign," Lonnie said, and dropped the flake to the snow. The horse leaned down and continued to eat and Lonnie went back to the truck and drove it up past the main mine, turned it around, and drove back to the assayer's office. He opened the stock trailer door and took the lead rope from Al. On his first try he led the horse into the trailer. He tied the halter rope to a ring that hung from the front wall and shut the trailer door.

"How did you do that?" Al asked.

"It wasn't me. He just knows what he's doing." Lonnie shook the snow from his hat and put it back on. "What I'm thinking is we drive him to Tonopah. There's a dog vet there and he'll know what to do about the eyes and the fucked-up leg, at least. The real horse vet is out of Bishop. It might take him a couple days to get here depending how busy he is. If the dog vet isn't around, we'll call Bishop and drive over there unless this storm doesn't quit. But I got to tell you, it's gonna cost you some money."

"I'll pay whatever it takes," Al said.

"Well, the poor guy's gonna have a shit-ass time going down the road but I guess it's better than living next to a dead coyote and being stuck out here listening to Mormon radio and eating spaghetti." He turned back to Al. "But before we go, man, we got to have a talk. I ain't gonna bullshit you, Al. You're getting that face people in concentration camps got, sucked in and hopeless. I've known you for almost four years and this is the first time I've seen you look like what you should look like, living out here by yourself. And you're drinking and you've told me time and time again you can't drink anymore. And you haven't looked after your car and I'm guessing you don't have enough wood to last the winter because I didn't leave you enough because there could never be enough with that piece-of-shit old broken woodstove. All of it says to me that you want to die but then I don't think you want to die, either. So you're just in that ditch . . . What I'm saying is you should come back with me. Besides Tex and Teresa, I got another plan. Like I told you, Sammi and I are in the main house for the next couple months, getting it ready for the new owners. In the meantime I want to set you up in the bunkhouse while I redo it. We'll get you on your feet again and get your weight better. I'd say you could stay in the main house, but Sammi and I barely know each other and I want to stay in bed as much as possible. You know what I mean? And then when you're feeling up to it, I think you should move back to Reno and start dating Teresa. That's what I'd do, any-way . . . But to do that, we got to get your weight back up and get you to a barber. You can't look the way you look now. You'd scare the shit out of her. If you're gonna bitch and want to stay here, then the only way I'll let you is if you get a better woodstove and a four-wheeler. And even with that you'll have to come back with me to wait out winter. You look too bad for me to leave you here. I wouldn't feel right. I mean I don't want to kidnap you, but you're weak as shit and it would be pretty easy."

Al stared at the assayer's shack. "I don't want to live here anymore, Lonnie . . . I knew it was a mistake from the first day I got here, I just didn't know what else to do."

"Well, it's over now." Lonnie looked at him and smiled. "I say before you change your mind, let's get what you need and get the fuck out of here before we get stuck. The snow's really dumping now. We'll come back for the rest later. All right?"

Al nodded and they went to the shack. He packed a suitcase with his clothes and toiletries. He grabbed the Telecaster from underneath his bed and the *Atlas of the Breeding Birds of Nevada*. Lonnie brought the classical guitar, the broken recliner, and the radio that was on the side of the road. They put it all in the bed of the truck and covered it with a tarp.

Al then walked up to the mine. Inside the shaft he came to the gray metal ammunition box and opened it. He grabbed a plastic Ziploc of photos and took out one of Maxine in pajamas sitting by a Christmas tree on Christmas Day, one of Mel at the mine's entrance, one of Vern sitting next to the Truckee River in swim trunks, and one of The Sanchez Brothers band standing on the steps of the Motown Museum in Detroit. He put the photos in his coat pocket and put the rest back. He walked farther into the mine and came to the green ammunition box. Inside was another Ziploc with six thousand dollars in hundreds and his last bottle of Centenario. He put the money in his coat, put the tequila under his arm, and went back to the assayer's office. He grabbed the cardboard box with his spiral notebooks and locked the door. For a long time he stood on the porch and looked out at the broken beauty of the place. Even then, in the condition he was in, half of him begged not to leave.

Lonnie drove and Al looked at the assayer's office until it disappeared behind him. The truck slid and struggled and the horse knocked around in the old stock trailer, but they made it through the canyon and the foothills and came to the valley. Lonnie took off his cowboy hat and ran his hands through his hair. He turned the radio back on and they headed toward Tonopah. Al looked at the photos he'd taken from the mine and then grabbed the bottle of tequila at his feet, opened it, and took a sip. He handed the bottle to Lonnie, who also took a drink.

"What happened to you after Gerry sold the ranch?" Al asked. "How did you end up in Douglas, and what happened to your leg?"

Lonnie began chewing on his nails again. "If it's okay, I don't want to talk about that right now. Gerry just never paid me what he owed me and the truck he gave me had a fucked-up title. A lot of bad luck, man. And then after that . . . Well . . . Everything went wrong. I'll tell you about it sometime when you're feeling better and I'm used to feeling better."

"I'm sorry I didn't help you."

"It's all right. You didn't know."

"You've been a good friend to me and I should have known."

"At least we're both okay now."

Al looked at the black-and-white photo of Maxine. "And at least we've both been in love," he said. "That's pretty lucky in a guy's life. To know how that feels." He took another drink and looked out the windshield.

"It is," Lonnie said. "Even if it blows up."

"Even if it blows up," Al whispered. "You know, my whole life I've been the same, Lonnie. And I've tried to change. I really have. I . . . I thought as I got older I'd figure more things out, but the truth is I haven't figured much out . . . My nerves seem like they've always been shot and that don't look like it'll ever go away. And since my early twenties I've never been able to completely quit drinking. That motherfucker has always been around my neck and I've . . . I've never really been at ease anywhere. At least not for very long. Even running away, even out here, I couldn't escape that. Even when I was in love."

"It takes a lot of energy to change who you are," Lonnie said.

"Yeah . . ."

"You gotta remember, Al, anyone would be a suicidal maniac living out here on their own. And it ain't like you're that fucked up, anyway. You're in your, what, mid-sixties?"

"Yeah."

"And you ain't killed yourself yet or gone completely nuts. And for the four years I've known you out here, every time I drove up to see you, you were dressed to the nines, clean-shaven, using that Italian aftershave shit, wearing your rings and the silver watch. And you were cool to me. You gave me good advice, and shit, man, you listened when I told you about my brother. You listened when I was bawling like a kid. That really helped. And you've given me way too much money . . . I mean why do you think people live in cities in the first place? It's because people go nuts living by themselves. Everybody in the world knows that."

"Yeah."

"But still, you did it."

"Yeah." Al took another drink and handed the bottle back to Lonnie.

"At least you saved a horse, Al. That's something. If you were dead, if you weren't alive, you wouldn't have saved him. He'd still be there freezing his ass off, trying not to get attacked by coyotes. And who knows, maybe at one time he was a great horse. Maybe at one time he was a cutting horse as good as Smart Little Lena or as fast as Dash for Cash. You just don't know who somebody is. So to me, if all you ever did in your whole life was walk thirty miles to save an old horse, well, shit, that's something, ain't it? That says something. Most people wouldn't cross the street to do something decent, and you walked thirty miles in the snow, and you're a drunk, lazy musician."

Al laughed. "Will the horse be all right?"

"I ain't a vet but he seems okay to me. He's got good gut sounds and he was eating. He can walk. Most likely he'll just be an expensive lawn ornament. He can stay with me if you pay for the hay and keep."

"I'll pay," Al said. "Thank you for that and for remembering me, Lonnie."

"Shit, I've always liked you, Al. You're a cool old-timer, and I get it, I do. It's a dark world if you open your eyes at all and aren't a dumb shit or a Bible-thumping Mormon. But for now I'm gonna try and keep mine as shut as possible because I have Sammi and I don't want to mess that up. And you should keep yours closed, too, because you have Tex and he's just a kid and he deserves a good life. And, of course, your horse," Lonnie said, and handed the bottle back to Al. "Shit, in less than a day you picked up two mouths to feed, so you better shape up."

Al again laughed.

"I got a question for you, Al."

"What's that?"

"While we've been driving, I've been thinking. I bet you'll probably write a song about the horse. Am I right?"

Al sat up in the seat. "It's interesting you said that, Lonnie, because while I was walking to find you, I thought of a couple ideas that could work. I'm just not sure which angle yet . . . I'll probably have to write a few to get the right one."

ACKNOWLEDGMENTS

As always, I want to thank to my wife, Lee; my agent, Lesley Thorne; and my editor at Harper, Amy Baker, for helping this book see the light of day. I'd also like to thank my brother, JV. When I was thirteen he moved to Los Angeles and began sending me cassettes of bands he'd liked and radio stations he listened to. Those cassettes of X, Los Lobos, Rank & File, and the Blasters changed my life. One of my favorite memories comes from a club in LA called the Palace. My brother had snuck me in to see Rank & File when I was fifteen. The band played, he had his arm around me, and let me drink his beer. I wish I could live inside that moment forever.

As I worked on *The Horse* four songwriters kept coming to mind. I've been a fan of John Doe for over forty years, and I can't think of a better musician to dedicate this book to. He's a friend whose records have been an inspiration to me for most of my life. Dallas Good is also a real hero of mine. People always ask if you could be in any band what band would it be? The Stones, The Stooges, Rush, The Minutemen, Black Sabbath, The Clash? I always say the same thing: The Sadies. Watching Dallas and his brother Travis play guitars together was heaven to me. Patterson Hood and Scott McCaughey are two of my favorite songwriters and favorite people in the world. So much of *The Horse* was written thinking of them, how both have written songs for most of their lives. Through good runs and bad they have never stopped.

Last but definitely not least, I've been so fortunate that

Harper has believed in me for as long as they have. Amy Baker is pure aces. Thanks also to Virginia Stanley, Lainey Mays, Bob Alunni, Beth Thomas, and Tom Hopke. Milan Bozic did a brilliant job designing such a beautiful cover, and special thanks also to Gabe, Jim, Ronnie, and all the Harper reps for taking care of me, and to everyone at Harper for helping my novels make their way into the world.

ABOUT THE AUTHOR

WILLY VLAUTIN is the author of the novels *The Motel Life, Northline, Lean on Pete, The Free, Don't Skip Out on Me,* and *The Night Always Comes.* He is the founding member of the bands Richmond Fontaine and The Delines. He lives outside Portland, Oregon.